guys, dating, and sex

The Girls' Guide to Relationships

Tammy Bennett

Revell
Grand Rapids, Michigan

Published by Fleming H. Revell
a division of Baker Publishing Group
P.O. Box 6287, Grand Rapids, MI 49516-6287

Printed in the United States of America

Library of Congress Cataloging-in-Publication Data
Bennett, Tammy.
    Guys, dating, and sex : the girls' guide to relationships / Tammy Bennett.
        p.   cm.
    ISBN 0-8007-3082-8 (pbk.)
    1. Man-woman relationships. 2. Man-woman relationships—Religious aspects—Christianity. 3. Dating (Social customs) 4. Dating (Social customs)—Religious aspects—Christianity. 5. Sex. 6. Sex—Religious aspects—Christianity. 7. Sexual abstinence. 8. Sexual ethics for teenagers. I. Title.
HQ801.B473 2005
241'.6765—dc22   2005001978

interior design by Brian Brunsting

This book is dedicated to my son.

Dear Matthew, I pray that you will grow into a man of great wisdom and integrity. I love you. Mom

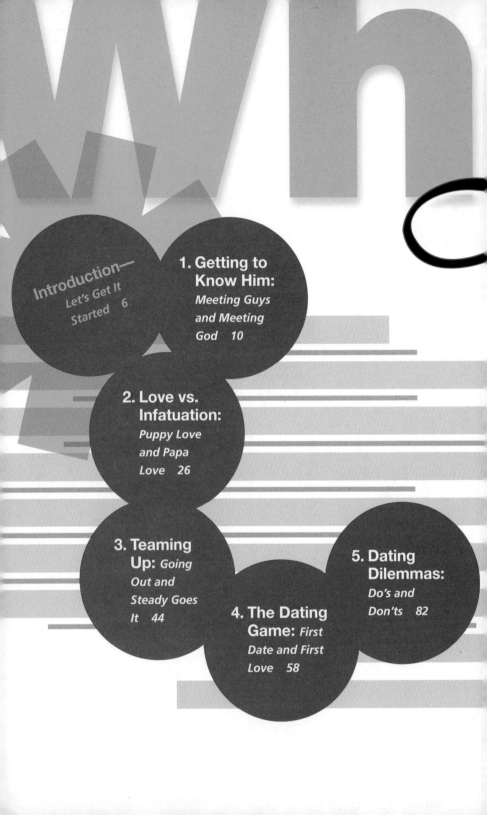

at's

Inside

Introduction

Let's Get It Started

Hey, girlfriend! Good to be with you again, and to my new readers, welcome! Here we are in book number three . . . everything you need to know about *Guys, Dating, and Sex.*

That's right, this book is all about boys, relationships, and that little three-letter word with the humongous meaning, S-E-X!

> **Guys**—who they are, what they are, their likes and dislikes, and most of all how they do or do not relate to us as girls
>
> **Dating**—the whys and why nots, ups and downs, pros and cons, and everything in between
>
> **Sex**—why we should wait, why we often don't and wish we had, and the consequences that follow the act

Have you ever noticed that guys are different? Yes, it's true, they are not only different physically but they are also wired different emotionally. They are more than the opposite sex; they are irreplaceable individuals created to balance our female makeup. In other words, as crazy as they make us and no matter how immature or insensitive they might come across, we're still attracted to their masculine characteristics.

I remember my first crush—stalking him in the school hallways, asking my friends to find out who he liked, arranging accidental encounters, and doodling his name all over my folder. Every waking moment was consumed with him, the man of my dreams, my one and only . . . well, that is, until the next crush came around. Starting in middle school I was gaga over guys. But the fact is, I didn't understand them from the start. I didn't have a clue how to impress them or get their attention or how to know the difference between true love and infatuation.

I remember once liking this guy with braces on his teeth. His flashy smile sent shivers up and down my spine. There was only one little problem with our relationship . . . it was one-sided. He didn't know I existed. I tried everything to get his attention; finally I resorted to drastic measures. I constructed my own retainer to wear across my teeth using a paperclip and a piece of plastic. For some reason I thought braces would be our common bond. The next day I saw him sitting in the school library and courageously went in and sat down at his table. He instantly looked up, wondering who was invading his privacy, and I flashed him my own mock metal smile. And guess what—it got his attention. He actually spoke to me. "Hey, when did you get your braces off? I get mine off next week. I hope my teeth straightened out better than yours so I don't have to wear a dumb retainer." Yep, that was a magic moment all right. One that made me want to die right there on the spot. I felt like such a geek. Needless to say, that relationship went nowhere fast; my crush had crushed me. It was hopeless. Not even braces could bring us together.

Why do guys make us do such *stupid, stupid* things? It's like they walk by and we lose our senses trying to chase after them. We'll stoop to any level to be noticed by some of the biggest losers out there. We often sell ourselves short in order to win over someone we really shouldn't have wanted in the first place.

Well, girl, it's time to change all that and get smarter where guys are concerned. It's time to learn what the Bible says about guys, dating, and sex so we can focus on what really matters: letting relationships happen the way God intended. We need to turn our attention to the main man, focusing on our relationship with the one and only Jesus Christ. We should be committed to Christ first and foremost, and then use that relationship as a model for all others. When we get our vertical relationship on track, all of our horizontal relationships will fall into place—relationships with our parents, siblings, friends, and yes, even guys.

> But more than anything else, put God's work first and do what he wants. Then the other things will be yours as well.
>
> Matthew 6:33 CEV

Believe it or not, God created the opposite sex and our innate attraction to them. Here's something else that might shock you: God created sex! And as the inventor, he has given us explicit directions on how, when, where, and why it should be experienced.

Hmmm . . . guys, dating, and sex . . . sound too complicated, creepy, and confusing? Well, today's your lucky day! I'm about to enlighten you with everything you need to know about making good decisions so you can avoid the consequences that follow bad judgment. I'm even going to tell you what your mother wanted to explain to you but couldn't. So if you're ready to learn what's opposite about the opposite sex, how to set the date for a date, why sex and sexy mean only one thing, and how God relates to all of the above, let's get started!

Your friend,

Tammy

• •

Be TRUE to YOU—Center feelings of love on information rather than infatuation to eliminate mixed emotions.

1

Getting

to
Know
Him

Guys . . . have you ever wondered about them? What makes them tick and act the way they do? Or better yet, have you ever questioned your own behavior around them? Why do you get squeamish, stutter, and giggle?

It's like one day they totally grossed you out, infecting you with cooties, and then all of a sudden, without warning, they invaded your brain, and now you find yourself with males on your mind. Of course, some of us are more boy-crazy than others, but the fact is, at some point in our lives most of us are bitten by the boy bug. And once the love bug bites . . . well, girlfriend, that's when the troubles begin. The truth is, girls are not like guys and vice versa. Males and females are opposite in many ways. Aside from the obvious physical differences, they are also different mentally and emotionally.

The good news is that girl/guy relationships get a lot less complicated when we take time to know the rules before we dive in. To be successful in a competition you need to know not only how to play the game but also your opponent, as well as your own strengths and weaknesses. The same is true in the dating game: a little bit of know-how gives you the upper hand so that you don't enter the battle of the sexes haphazardly, depending solely on luck.

Play it smart. When it comes to guys, dating, and sex, it's best to be in the know now instead of wishing you had known better before you got started down the wrong path.

It's time to get to know more about boys, and to do that we are going to learn about ourselves first. Knowing how we are made up will help us better understand why we're physically, emotionally, and mentally attracted to guys. Have you ever found yourself wondering, "Why do guys make girls act

Getting to Know Him

goofy?" Well, the fact is, that's the way God designed us. It all started with Adam and Eve back in the Garden of Eden and has progressed to where we are today. And although the times have changed—here's a little secret—the need for companionship has not. Each of us hopes to find true love at some point in our lives, but the question is: where should we begin the search? The answer? Start within yourself.

It's All about Knowing ME

Choices. Our lives are filled with choices, and one of the biggest of all, one that has the potential to affect us for life, is the one we make where guys are concerned. Even though the stats show that the girl-to-guy ratio is almost two to one, the selection of guys can still seem mind-boggling. In some respects it even makes the good old Bible days sound appealing! Think about it. Eve had no choice. Even though there were *literally* a lot of fish in the sea, there was only one man to choose from—Adam. How lucky was she? No dating or being dumped; just one guy, one gal, and one Creator. And then from the days of Adam and Eve, we moved into numerous generations of prearranged marriages, which still exist in some places today. And although that may have its perks, the majority of us would rather do the choosing ourselves. The question is *How?* Where should you start? The answer, surprisingly enough, is not found in who you choose but in who the choice is for—the answer is found in you!

Get a Clue

To know what you want, you must know what you are looking for and learn not to settle for anything less. Most likely quite a few guys will come and go out of your life before you happen upon Mr. Right, and you don't want any encounters with the Mr. Wrongs to have damaging results before you find him. Although we doodle hearts to signify romance, it's our heads that need to sensibly think us through it. To be successful you need to play it smart by knowing who you are and what you want out of life. Use this questionnaire to help you get started:

Always remember you're someone special. You should never settle for second best. The best guy complements who you are, respects you, values you, and NEVER pressures you to do anything you don't want to do or be anything you are not.

Getting to Know Me

Date: Dec. 26/05

My favorite hobbies and/or activities are:
Basketball, Volleyball, singing, reading

My hopes and dreams consist of:
I hope me and Jason will always be together.

This is what makes me feel best about myself and gives me a boost of self-esteem:
People are always complementing my red hair and that makes me feel good.

This is what my friends and family mean to me:
I know I wouldn't be able to survive without them and I'm always thankful for their guidence.

My future plans consist of (for example, college or career):
I would definately like to go to college and maybe get a bachelor in science.

Things I can't stand:

People chewing loudly, Girls with big mouth that think they know everything—

Must-have qualities in a husband:

Christain, rich, romantic, funny.

How I want to be treated as a wife:

I want to always be needed.

This is what I plan to accomplish before I get married (for example, high school, college, career, travel . . .):

Get through highschool, college and have a steady career.

After you make your list, put it in a place where you can read it and revise it as needed. There's nothing magic about keeping a list; it just helps you be more aware of who you are and what you want out of life. For example, if friends and/or family are important to you and your crush is overly possessive of your time, causing you to eliminate time with others, then you need to evaluate why you're compromising your standards in order to meet his. In a case like this you need to speak up and tell him how you feel, and if he gives you any flak simply say, "Adios, amigo!"

Simplify

Life is perplexing enough without making it more strenuous by bringing guys

Tammy's Tip

A good way to know all about yourself is to keep a diary that allows you to journal your innermost thoughts. Then from time to time reread it to get acquainted with you.

into it too fast or too soon. Keep things simple. Remember, boys who are friends are much easier to get along with and don't damage your self-esteem the way "boyfriends" can.

Take it slow. Don't rush romantic relationships with the opposite sex. You may feel that you're ready now, but let's get real for a moment. Fantasizing about happily-ever-after well before you're ready for marriage may be fun, but don't allow fiction to confuse the facts. The truth is, many girls just like you have compromised their long-term well-being for a few short-lived good times, and that's how statistics are born—on teen pregnancy, sexually transmitted diseases, emotional pain, and other issues.

Take a moment right now to commit yourself to your future before you commit yourself to someone who isn't worthy of you. It may sound silly, but many girls have changed what could have been with unwanted pregnancies, STDs, and emotional disorders. Without a focus, they lived for the moment instead of for what was awaiting them in their future.

Don't leave your tomorrows totally to chance. Take a moment right now and jot down what you are expectantly planning for. For example:

I plan on graduating from high school and attending college. Once I graduate from college, I will then consider marriage when the right guy comes along. I want to find a guy who loves God, adores me, and has a promising future.

I'm committed to saving my most precious gift, the present of my purity, for the one I marry. I will also respect my feelings and myself by protecting myself from being disrespected by others. I won't allow myself to be treated like a second-class citizen by anyone.

Write your own plans and commitments here:

Getting to Know Him

Date: **Dec. 26/05**

I Plan: **To finish college and definately consider marriage.**

I'm committed to: **definately saving sex for marriage. Duh!**

FYI

Life is a lot easier and much more fun when you like yourself—who you are and who you are becoming. The second most important relationship you need to have (the first being with Jesus Christ, which we will talk about later in this chapter) is with yourself. You need to be comfortable with knowing and accepting you from the inside out. True identity is not found in trying to find someone or something to identify with; true identity is established by knowing who you are and where you fit in naturally. It's not about being something you're not and trying to adapt to your surroundings; it's about being yourself and designing your environment around you. Girl, know that loving yourself from the inside out is not about being conceited but about being comfortable with who you are.

Too often girls find their identity in their clique of friends, the clothes they wear, the clubs or sports they take part in, or the guys they date. The sad part is that quite often their decisions are not based on personal opinion but instead swayed by popular opinion. It's called **peer pressure**. It's what persuades us to be who we are not and do what we wouldn't normally do. It's when others knowingly or unknowingly force their influence upon us. Peer pressure weighs us down big-time, and the only way to lighten the load is by also carrying a healthy amount of self-esteem. Respect yourself, your likes and dislikes, your needs and wants, and your hopes and dreams. *Like who you are* and others will like you too!

"No one can make you feel inferior without your consent."

Eleanor Roosevelt

Getting to Know Him

What's It 2U?

Getting to know you is the most important part of understanding how you relate to others and how others relate to you. The key to having successful relationships is having a good relationship with yourself first, because when you learn to like yourself, others will like you too. And when you're comfortable with yourself, you won't need to find your identity in superficial relationships that aren't right for you. Your identity will be established not in who you know but in who you know you are. That's key to setting healthy boundaries for yourself and others who associate with you. Girls who develop self-confidence define themselves now so they won't be redefined later by consequences such as unexpected pregnancies, drug addiction, abortion, or HIV. Don't be caught off guard. Plan today for better tomorrows.

C4 Yourself

The game of life can be challenging enough without living haphazardly and leaving everything to chance. Some risks are worth taking, like risking your own reputation to befriend someone who's less than popular at school, but some are ridiculous gambles, like having casual sex and risking a lifetime of regret. Be smart, not sorry. Live your life with purpose. Live your life with you and your future in mind.

Meeting God

Have you ever questioned God? Who he is, where he is, and if he cares? Or have you ever wondered who you are in relationship to him?

The questions about God never end, and I definitely won't pretend to have all the answers. But I'm excited to share what

I do know to be true. Yes, there is one, and *only* one, true God. He has always existed and always will. He's all-powerful and can do absolutely anything (except sin or tempt someone to sin). He is everywhere all the time and knows everything about all things simultaneously. He knows you—what you think, what you feel, and what you do. He even knows exactly how many hairs are on your head at any given moment. God is completely perfect in every way. I could go on and on about his attributes—his goodness, faithfulness, holiness, righteousness, and on and on—but my explanation wouldn't begin to describe what only you can experience personally: his grace.

God's grace and mercy are available to anyone, anywhere, 24/7. He loves you unconditionally; however, the decision is yours whether or not you will love him back. Can I tell you a secret? *God's got a crush on you!* He'd like nothing more than to have a personal relationship with you through his Son Jesus Christ (JC). What about you? Would you like to know how to hook up with God? I hope you'll say yes, because I guarantee you that this is the one relationship you will be eternally happy you got into.

Knowing about God covers an infinite amount of information, more than I could ever know or share. But knowing God on an intimate level is something I know all about from my own personal experience. Allow me to explain. *Knowing about* someone is way different than *knowing* them personally. I know about many famous people—their likes, dislikes, dog's name, birthplace, favorite color, etc.—but I don't know them personally, and they do not know me. That's what it means to know about someone. To *know* someone means that you are acquainted with

Cater to who you are, not to who someone else wants you to be.

Tammy's Tip

If you don't like something about yourself, change it, downplay it, or work with it. For example, you can change a bad habit, downplay large thighs, or work with limp hair. Remember, others will respond favorably to you when you are happy with yourself.

that person on a personal level, like you know your very best friend, for instance. Although *know about* and *know* may seem similar in meaning, they are as far as the east is from the west when you consider them in light of who you are in relationship to God.

God did not create us to know about him, but to be known by him.

It's All about Knowing God

Believe it or not, it is possible to simply know all about a relationship with Christ without accepting him into your life. It all comes down to one simple question: do you *know* God with your heart or do you *know about* God with your head? Head knowledge or heart knowledge, that is the question. Now let's talk about the response. Pay close attention because this is one answer that makes the difference between eternal security in heaven or an endless time in hell.

Get a Life

Like the guy/girl relationship thing, this whole problem with knowing versus knowing about God started in the Garden of Eden, with Adam and Eve. Maybe you remember the story. God created everything, including a magnificent garden for Adam and Eve to live in, with all the food they could ever ask for. They needed nothing and had everything—except the fruit of one certain tree growing right smack-dab in the middle of the garden, the tree of the knowledge of good and evil, which God had set off-limits. Everything was going just fine until Satan entered the scene cleverly disguised as a serpent and tricked Eve into tasting the forbidden fruit. She ate it and then passed it along to Adam, who had some too. Interestingly enough, the first bit of knowledge they gained was that they were naked and needed to cover themselves up with clothes, which they busily started sewing together out of fig leaves.

Next thing you know, God came strolling through the garden, looking for them, already knowing they were hiding out because they had done what they were not supposed to do. Finally Adam acknowledged God's presence, came out of hiding, and instantly started playing the blame game. Adam first blamed God for giving him this woman and then went on to blame Eve for giving him the fruit to eat. Next Eve, realizing she was now in the hot seat, pointed her finger at the serpent. No one wanted to take the blame, but it didn't matter because the damage was already done. The result was that sin entered the world, followed by death and separation from God. It all started with one man, Adam, and was passed on to all generations to follow, including yours and mine.

> The sin of this one man, Adam, caused death to rule over us, but all who receive God's wonderful, gracious gift of righteousness will live in triumph over sin and death through this one man, Jesus Christ. Yes, Adam's one sin brought condemnation upon everyone, but Christ's one act of righteousness makes all people right in God's sight and gives them life. Because one person disobeyed God, many people became sinners. But because one other person obeyed God, many people will be made right in God's sight.
>
> Romans 5:17–19 NLT

The bottom line is that ever since Adam, we all have sinned, and we all have received the same judgment—separation from God. Yes, we inherited Adam's sinful nature, but along with that we also inherited Adam's free will. Now here's the cool part. With that free will we have the right to choose our own destiny; we have the right to choose whether or not we want a relationship with God through his Son Jesus Christ. He does not impose

Tammy's Tip

No religion, rules, regulations, or rituals can possibly compare to a personal RELATIONSHIP with Jesus Christ.

himself on anyone. God wants a relationship only with those who want a relationship with him. He won't force you, but he longs for you to take the information you *know about* him in your head and apply it to your heart so that you can *know* him on a personal level.

The Simple Truth

Here's what we know so far:

1. Everyone has sinned, including you and me.

   "For all have sinned; all fall short of God's glorious standard" (Rom. 3:23 NLT).

   Sin is a fancy word for anything we do wrong, covering everything from bad thoughts to attitudes, and behavior.

2. The penalty for our sin is death—separation from God forever.

   "When people sin, they earn what sin pays—death. But God gives us a free gift—life forever in Christ Jesus our Lord" (Rom. 6:23 NCV).

   The death Scripture is talking about here is spiritual death, separation from God forever. Although our earthly bodies die, our souls, or who we are on the inside, live on forever. The question is where—heaven? Or hell? The answer lies in whether or not you choose to receive God's gift.

3. You can't earn this present, so don't even try.

   "You were saved [from death] by faith in God, who treats us much better than we deserve. This is God's gift to you, and not anything you have done on your own. It isn't something you have earned, so there is nothing you can brag about" (Eph. 2:8–9 CEV).

   Unfortunately, many people believe they must earn their way to heaven by doing good deeds, giving money to the poor, going to church, and that kind of thing, but the GOOD NEWS is, that's just not true. According to the Bible we can do nothing ourselves but accept God's free gift of salvation.

FYI

Can I share one more thing? This is really important to think about. *Have you taken ownership of your relationship with God?* What I mean is, have you personally accepted Jesus as Lord of *your* life? Many times this is a confusing issue, especially for those who, like me, were raised going to church. It's easy to accept religious or moral practices without accepting Christ. I've talked to many teenagers who have followed their parents' faith without applying it to themselves. They may have been "good people," but when it came to a relationship with God, they were living vicariously, through their parents' or grandparents' faith. Take time to examine your own life right now. Have you accepted Jesus as *your own* personal Lord and Savior, or have you relied on what someone else believes? Again, this is the difference between *knowing about* God and *knowing* God personally.

What's It 2U?

Still not sure you're ready to commit? Well, trust me, this is one love connection you don't want to miss out on. Guys will come and go in your life, but God will never leave you, not even for one fleeting second.

> God assured us, "I'll never let you down, never walk off and leave you."
>
> Hebrews 13:5–6 Message

He'll hang with you through thick and thin, good and bad, better and worse, everywhere and everything. He'll *NEVER* let you down. How do I know this? I can testify to his faithfulness because I know him personally. But the question is, do you?

Getting to Know Him

C4 Yourself

Who you are in relationship to God is the most important thing you'll ever consider. But don't mull it over too long, because some risks are worth taking and some are not. Every day we live with the assumption that we have tomorrow, the next day, and the day after that, but in reality we have no guarantees about even the next hour. This afternoon I went to have my nails done, and while I was there I sat at the nail dryer next to a girl who was visibly upset. I asked her what was wrong, and with tears in her eyes she shared that she had been notified that day that her friend, who was only seventeen, had been killed in a car accident the night before.

Time Out
with Tammy

I grew up going to church three times a week. I sat through endless hours of Sunday school, learning about God's Word without understanding how it applied directly to me. I kept hearing about being "saved" and having "eternal security," but didn't know what it meant or where to get it. Finally I started to understand that I needed to be saved, so I went to the pastor for some answers. He explained the whole sin thing to me—the fact that I was a sinner (Rom. 3:23) and why my sin separated me from God (Rom. 6:23). He told me that there was nothing I could do on my own except receive God's gift to me (Eph. 2:8–9). And then he reached into the lower left side drawer of his desk and pulled out a beautifully wrapped package. He held out the present toward me and said, "This is the gift of God's Word to you. All you have to do is believe it and accept it as your very own." "Believe what?" I asked. The pastor said, "Believe the Christmas story. Do you believe Luke 1 and 2, where it tells us that God sent his Son to be born of the Virgin Mary?" I nodded my head yes. Next he asked if I believed in the Easter story. "Do you believe that Jesus died on the cross for your sins? Do you believe that he was buried and rose again according to the Scriptures and that he now lives in heaven with God the Father? Do you believe John 3:16?"

John 3:16 says, "For God so loved the world that he gave his one and only Son [Jesus], that whoever believes in him shall not perish but have eternal life."

"Yes, I believe," I said, and I reached out and accepted the present he was handing me. I quickly untied the fancy white ribbon and tore off the red wrapping, which

Getting to Know Him

Girl, I'm warning you, don't live in the land of assumption, taking for granted that you'll be able to choose a relationship with God at a later date. A time will come when it will be too late to commit, and I hope that you don't find out when that time is without being ready. Don't put off God for another second. Now is the time to say "I do" to God. God did his part—through his grace and mercy, he provided you with eternal life through his Son, Jesus. Now it's up to you to receive it. Life is stressful, but Christ wants to be your eternal-life partner and empower you through it. It's all up to you. What will you do? You can be a risk-taker or take a chance on God. The choice is yours. Will you say "I do"?

Be TRUE to YOU—Accept God's proposal for a "happily-ever-after"

exposed a shiny, new, silver Bible. The pastor told me, "You've now accepted the gift of God's Word, literally and figuratively. Now there's only one thing to do: pray."

Romans 10 says, "For if you confess with your mouth that Jesus is Lord and believe in your heart that God raised him from the dead, you will be saved. For it is by believing in your heart that you are made right with God, and it is by confessing with your mouth that you are saved. . . . For 'Anyone who calls on the name of the Lord will be saved'" (verses 9–10, 13 NLT). So at that moment I bowed my head and prayed something similar to this:

> Dear God,
> I know that I have done things that are wrong and that I can't do anything about it on my own except believe and accept that Jesus died on the cross for my sins. Please forgive me of my sins and be part of my life. Thank you for saving me and for giving me the Bible.
> In Jesus's Name,
> Amen

It was that simple, and my life hasn't been the same since. Sure, I've had ups and downs throughout life just like everyone else, but the difference is that I can rely on God to help me through it. A personal relationship with God brings new meaning to everything . . . even guys, dating, and sex. If you don't know God, I hope you will use the prayer above to express your desire to have your own personal relationship with him.

2 Love

vs. Infatuation

Puppy Love

"And they called it puppy love . . ." A Donny Osmond song I loved, but an expression I hated when it referred to my latest crush and me. Although I never quite understood what it all had to do with puppies, I knew the term made light of my emotions. I didn't like being teased about my feelings towards the opposite sex. I knew in my own heart that not every boyfriend could be "the one," yet I liked romanticizing the possibility. Infatuation does that to us. Infatuation, in many ways, makes us act foolish even when we know better. The question is how can we avoid being played the fool in the process? How should we respond to infatuation? Should we ignore it and hope it goes away or act on it? What should you do when your head says no but your heart says yes?

In this chapter we are going to find out more about puppy love and figure out how to handle it. Guys, like puppies, come in many breeds, shapes, and sizes; so many are cute and adorable that choosing just one to commit to can be a difficult decision to make. And often instead of waiting until we're ready, we move from guy to guy hoping one will stand out from the rest of the litter. Yet the question is, how involved in a relationship should you get before you realize this just isn't the pup for you? Understanding the differences between love and infatuation is key to avoiding the hurt and hardship that come from locking yourself into a relationship you're not ready for. The next few pages will help you set healthy boundaries between you and the male species. After all, you don't want to get stuck with a Chihuahua when the man of your dreams is more like a Great Dane.

Love vs. Infatuation

Love grows, infatuation dies, and puppy love is better left to animal lovers.

Have you ever known anyone who picked out a puppy and brought it home only to find out they were not ready for the responsibility that came with it? They unleashed their emotions, and before you know it, they committed themselves to something they were not ready for. Romantic puppy love does the same thing to us. It attacks our feelings, making us love-obsessed, which often puts us into compromising situations we're not ready for. Our emotions trick us into thinking it will last forever when in reality, forever usually turns into a few short weeks at best.

Will It Last?

Will it last? Hmmm . . . statistics indicate . . . NO! Only about 20 percent of high school romances end in marriage, and only 4 percent of those marriages last. So the chances of your high school sweetheart becoming your lifelong (until you're in your eighties) mate are really slim. You need to understand what this says about relationships in your teen years so you don't mess up your future. It's all about setting healthy boundaries. Apply the truth now so you don't have to suffer the consequences later.

Get a Clue

Knowing the differences between physical attraction and emotional involvement will help you avoid mistakes. I want to make something perfectly clear. This is sooooooo important. Here it is: *guys and girls are different!* No foolin', it's true. No matter how you look at it, males and females are not alike. They think differently, act differently, look differently, feel differently, and even shave differently. But all those differences are what we're attracted to, and those same

Love vs. Infatuation

differences are what
confuse us and get
us into trouble with
the opposite sex. In

**Sex is a physical act for guys
and an emotional act for girls.**

chapter 1 we talked about knowing you—who you are and
what you like—so now let's discuss guys and how you do or
do not relate to each other.

The male species is a breed all its own. They think, talk, and
tick in a whole different manner. They think in terms they
understand. Take the baseball analogy, for instance—when
guys think of and refer to their dates as a baseball game, it's
usually to say something like, "*Hey, I made it to second base
with Brooke last night.*" Girls, on the other hand, talk about
the emotional needs that were met on the date, like, "*I wore
my blue sweater, and he said blue is his favorite color. He took me to
the movies and held my hand the whole time, and we even shared
a bucket of popcorn with extra butter. He's so romantic.*" Get the
idea? Guys think in physical terms, and girls think with their
emotions.

And then there's guy talk. Most of them pretty much stick
to surface issues such as the weather, sports, and how souped-
up their cars are. In fact, they can pretty much communicate with a few grunts and get along fine. Guy 1: "*I hope the
weather doesn't throw my game off.*" Guy 2: "*Ah.*" (Translation:
"*Yeah, me too.*")

Girls, now, we're a whole different story. Unlike guys, most
of whom hardly ever utter a touchy-feely word, that's about
all girls do, and we tend to do it over lengthy conversations
that go into great detail. "*The rain makes me feel so depressed.
I hate having nothing to do, and I know Simon didn't call me and
invite me to watch his baseball game because he thinks I'm fat. Not
only that, but it seems like he wants to break up . . .*" Again let me
remind you, guys talk from a physical standpoint and girls
talk from an emotional standpoint.

Love vs. Infatuation

Finally there's what makes guys tick, and they are definitely "ticking to the beat of their own clock," so to speak. Guys are physical beings. Besides the fact that most never cease to be amused by their own physical bodily functions such as belching and farting, they also show their support on the ball fields by slapping and grabbing each other's tushes. Some guys can't even watch TV without acting out what they see. If they're watching wrestling, they'll wrestle each other to the ground, or if they're watching football, they'll be up on their feet, shouting wildly, coaching the game from the living room. I even know one guy who's really into golf, and every time I talk to him, he putts an invisible golf ball as he's trying to make his point in the conversation! It's almost like swinging the invisible golf club sets his brain into motion. Guys are physical beings, and they need and crave physical contact, but not in the same way girls do. We also get physical when we play sports; however, we are driven more by desires having to do with belonging, socializing, popularity, competitiveness, and perfection. Our emotional attitude, often controlled by a female hormone known as estrogen, drives our actions. This girly hormone plays on our emotions causing us to center our behavior on emotional response rather than physical act. Guys however are driven by the male hormone known as testosterone which causes guys to think, act, and relate differently. Bottom line, guys' and gals' chemical as well as physical makeup are different.

Knowing the physical and emotional differences between guys and girls will allow you to have good relationships with guys without taking them farther than they should go, especially in the area of sex. Listen up, this is important! If you don't get another thing from this book, get this:

Guys are physically stimulated and crave physical release; girls, on the

Tammy's Tip

Never put out more than you're willing to lose.

other hand, are emotionally moved and long for emotional fulfillment. To guys, sex is a matter of care, which is not to be confused with love. "*If you care for me you will . . .*" To guys, care relates to a physical need being met, but to girls care is defined as an emotion linked to the warm fuzzy feelings of being in love. Yes, males and females even have their own emotional and physical responses to how they understand the definitions of words. This is vital information to consider as you start seeking out companionship with the opposite sex. Understanding each other's sexual makeup will protect you from emotional trauma that comes from misreading and getting over involved in relationships.

Simplify

Don't complicate your involvement with guys by introducing sexual encounters before it's time. You are going to be interested in many guys between now and when you get married. Believe me, the first guy that comes along will not be the last, so don't let him have you first.

FYI

I read this great book called *Dateable: Are You? Are They?* by Justin Lookadoo and Hayley DiMarco (it was published by Revell in 2003). I highly recommend reading it if you haven't already. In it they give great information on what being *Dateable* is all about for both guys and girls. In the first chapter they give a formula to determine how many crushes you'll probably have before you get married. They wrote:

> The average age people get married is 25. So take 25 and subtract your age. We'll call your answer "years left" (see formula below). That's how many years you have left, on

average, before you marry. Now, write down how many crushes you have had in the last 12 months. Got it? Now take the number of crushes and multiply it by your "years left." The number you get is the number of crushes you will have before you get married.

$$25 - \underline{14} = \underline{11}$$
$$\text{your age} \quad \text{years left}$$

$$\underline{5} \times \underline{11} = \underline{55}$$
number of crushes   years left   number of crushes
last 12 months   'til you find "the one"

Did you plug in your numbers and complete the formula? Hope so. This will give you a realistic idea of how many times you're going to pretend to commit before the real "I do" pledge comes along. Yes, I am aware that this statistic won't always be true, but for the great majority it is. This should help you understand why your mom doesn't dive into wedding preparations every time you come home and announce your latest love. She already knows that sooner or later your latest love is going to be your last love when the next love comes along. My advice? Start a relationship knowing that it's going to end. Following this basic rule of thumb will save you from the emotional trauma of having invested too much when puppy love fades away.

What's It 2U?

Q. Should I ignore puppy love?
A. Not necessary. Just don't indulge yourself in it too much.

Q. Should I encourage puppy love?
A. I wouldn't encourage or discourage puppy love because it's a natural part of growing up.

Tammy's Tip

Don't end up crushed by thinking your crush will last forever.

Love vs. Infatuation

However, the important thing to remember is that it's not forever, and you may fall out of infatuation as quickly as you were swept away by it.

Q. Should I act on puppy love?
A. This depends whether or not you can handle it. Are you able to have a boyfriend without getting intimate? If the answer is "no," then don't act on it. But if you can enter into it with boundaries, knowing this isn't the only guy you're ever going to like, then by all means, go for it.

There's no surefire way to stop puppy love, but there are methods of dealing with it logically. If your head says no but your heart says yes, make a list of the pros and cons of dating him to help you see if he's a good guy for you before you leave part of your heart behind and end up hurt.

C4 Yourself

Puppy love is very real, and when it ends it can leave you feeling hurt, confused, and abandoned. Infatuation creates feelings of love and devotion while it lasts, but quite often when it dies it eats away at our self-esteem. Sometimes when a guy would break up with me, I would sulk and wonder what was wrong with me, when in reality it wasn't him or me—it was just a bad match. Protect yourself from heartbreak by starting every relationship with the understanding that it's only temporary. Keeping this in mind will help you say no to an intimate relationship even if the guy and conditions seem right at the time. Don't confuse love with infatuation, and remember, you're going to experience many puppy loves before your top dog comes along.

● ● ● ● ● ● ● ● ● ● ● ● ● ● ● ● ● ● ● ●
No amount of puppy love
can add up to the real thing.

Love vs. Infatuation

Papa Love

There's nothing like being Daddy's little girl and having someone to love you, encourage you, and be there for you 24/7. Having that special father-daughter bond is a beautiful thing, and if you're fortunate enough to have that kind of relationship with your dad, be extremely thankful, because a lot of girls would love to be in your shoes. Sadly, way too many of us have no idea what it's like to experience a close relationship with our dads. Many of us have experienced abandonment, separation from divorce, or abuse, or we live under the same roof without communicating to one another. Those who live without a father's affection long for the total love and acceptance that only comes from a devoted daddy, and guess what? Even those girls who have a special bond with their earthly fathers still crave unconditional, doesn't-let-me-down, never-ending love that no human can supply.

A perfect relationship can only take place between you and your heavenly "Papa."

In this chapter we're going to look at what complete, unconditional love is, where it comes from, and how to receive it. This is the kind of love that your head doubts but your heart desperately seeks after. It's love of the purest and truest form; it's love from above, and it *only* comes from our heavenly Father. Unlike infatuation that's fleeting and human love that disappoints us, God's "Papa" love is forever and it never fails. So why do we ignore it instead of acting on it?

Take it from me, this is one relationship you don't want to live without. Others will disappoint you and let you down, but a relationship with the heavenly Father just keeps on giving and improves your life.

We are all born with a natural desire to love and be loved, and although our love is limited, we crave unlimited love. We long to have someone who knows everything there is

Love vs. Infatuation

to know about us and loves us anyway. We want someone who will accept us just the way we are, faults, failures, and all. We often try to find love of this magnitude in our relationships with family, friends, and boyfriends, and when it doesn't happen the way we expect it to, we feel rejected, like unlovable misfits. The problem is, we're looking for love in all the wrong places. There's only one place to look for a love like this, and that's up.

It Will Last

This resurrection life you received from God is not a timid, grave-tending life. It's adventurously expectant, greeting God with a childlike "What's next, Papa?" God's Spirit touches our

Time Out
with Tammy

When I was in third grade I was adopted, and although I didn't comprehend it at the time, I did experience a certain amount of rejection. Now, don't take what I'm saying the wrong way, because I was loved and provided for by my adopted dad. But I still couldn't help but wonder at first if he loved me or just loved my mom and accepted us as a package deal. You see, my mom's first husband, who was my birth father, abandoned us. Then my mom met and fell in love with the man who would marry her and adopt me. Although I settled into the relationship, I still wrestled with insecurity in the back of my mind. If anything happened between the two of them and they ended up divorced, I wondered, would I be dumped by another dad and up for adoption again? Although I felt loved, I longed to feel 100 percent secure in that love. What I really wanted was unconditional love—the kind of love no human can provide no matter how hard we try; the kind of unstoppable love that only comes from God.

What I didn't realize at the time was that God used my adoption experience to make me feel my need for eternal security in Christ. Only a couple of months after my earthly adoption, I prayed to receive Jesus and was adopted into the family of God. Third grade was a big year for me; I was adopted twice! First by the finest dad anyone could ask for on earth and next by our heavenly Father, an adoption that anyone, including you, can experience with one simple prayer.

spirits and confirms who we really are. We know who he is, and
we know who we are: Father and children. And we know we are
going to get what's coming to us—an unbelievable inheritance!

Romans 8:15–17 Message

Yes, this adoption will last for all eternity. Once you accept
God's gift of salvation by believing in and receiving his Son,
Jesus, you are a permanent member of the family of God.
He will never abandon you, neglect you, or turn a deaf ear
when you talk to him. He's there 24/7, listening, intervening,
encouraging, and delighting in your relationship with him.
And nothing can separate you from our heavenly Father's
never-ending love and devotion.

Get a Life

What's so cool about this adoption is that once you accept
Christ, you have a life—eternal life—and nothing can take
that away or change who you are in relationship to God.
You are the daughter of the King of Kings and Lord of Lords.
Congratulations! You are a princess and nothing, absolutely
nothing, can take that title away from you.

You belong to God. You are Daddy's little girl, and nothing will interfere with that fact. He will never run out on
you. Unlike infatuations that come and go, his love is here
to stay.

I used to think that God's love was condition-based because
I heard that our sin separated us from God. I was afraid that
every time I did something wrong, his affection for me was
terminated. I felt emotionally disconnected from God. But
what I didn't consider was
that I was the one who created the strain due to my
sin. It's kind of like this:

Tammy's Tip

Being adopted into the family of
God makes you his "relative"
through the blood of Christ.

Love vs. Infatuation

have you ever hurt someone and then felt strange being around him or her? I have, and the guilt I felt was overwhelming. The result was a shaky relationship until I sincerely apologized and received that person's forgiveness, and then our friendship reached a new level. It's the same with God: when we sin we hinder our relationship until we apologize and ask forgiveness, which then helps the relationship between Father and daughter mature and become even more beautiful.

The Simple Truth

The reason we don't experience God's unlimited love is that we don't allow ourselves that luxury. We've been programmed to believe love is performance based and hinges on our behavior. We think that we must say and do the right things in order to know and feel love. But the truth of the matter is, God loves you anytime, anywhere, every second of every day, and he wants you to experience his love wherever, whenever, in good times and bad. When we grow in God's love, we mature from thinking his love and acceptance are condition-based to a deeper understanding of his love for us, which makes us want to obey him. Remember, you are God's child not because of your love for him but because of his love for you.

> We love him, because he first loved us.
> 1 John 4:19 KJV

FYI

We have a deep desire for the kind of unconditional love and acceptance that only comes from God the Father. However, until we accept and receive it, we often try to fill that void with other relationships. When we're young we hope our parents or grandparents will meet all our needs, but when they disappoint us, we turn to friends and boyfriends. When those relationships aren't perfect either, we often over-commit in order to try to make them better. We want to be loved and accepted for who we are, but when that doesn't work, we morph into what others want us to be so that we can feel a sense of belonging.

I know that my own desires have caused me to do things that I never would have done if I wasn't looking for acceptance. I wanted so badly to be liked that I sold myself short in order to gain a sense of belonging. How about you? Have you buckled under peer pressure just to feel accepted? Tried alcohol? Drugs? Stealing? Cheating? Or have you gone further then you had intended with a guy, thinking that it would make him like you more so he wouldn't break up? A hunger to be loved unconditionally does that to us—it makes us overhaul our own lives in order to fit our warped sense of what it means to be loved unconditionally.

News flash: unconditional love can't be earned or manipulated; all you can do is accept it from God the way in which it is given. Remember, believing is receiving.

What's It 2U?

Q. Why do so many people ignore God's love?

A. People choose to ignore God's love for a variety of reasons, but one of the main ones is not feeling worthy of it. We don't think it's possible that God would love us for no reason whatsoever. We've been programmed to believe that anything worth having is earned. We are used to performance-based results, whether in love or anything else, so

Tammy's Tip

God loves you and pursued you first, hoping you would find it in your heart to accept his proposal.

Love vs. Infatuation

when we hear about a God who loves us just because, we find it hard to comprehend. The bottom line is, we've put conditions on *ourselves* that make us think God's love is unattainable. My advice is, stop trying to work for what you don't deserve, and just sit back and enjoy being loved by your heavenly Father, who deems you *extremely* worthy.

We can understand someone dying for a person worth dying for, and we can understand how someone good and noble could inspire us to selfless sacrifice. But God put his love on the line for us by offering his Son in sacrificial death while we were of no use whatever to him.

Romans 5:7–8 Message

Q. How can I apply God's love to my own life?
A. When you accept Christ into your life, you become a Christian, which can be interpreted as "to be Christlike." We each decide on a different vocation in life, such as doctor, designer, or dancer. But no matter the occupation, in order to know it, understand it, and perform it well, we must learn it and practice it. The same is true of Christianity. We choose to become Christians, and then we must study and practice what we learn. And the best place to gather information for this on-the-job training is your Bible. Read it and apply it, and you'll live a successful life as a Christian.

How can a young person live a clean life? By carefully reading the map of your Word.

Psalm 119:9 Message

But be doers of the word, and not hearers only.

James 1:22 NKJV

Q. How can I experience God's love anytime/anywhere?
A. Because God loves us and values us, he allows us to call on him 24/7 for help, advice, and encouragement that only he can give. You can pray every day, everywhere, every second of

every hour, and he'll hear every word. God is a good listener; the question is, are you? Sometimes we pray seeking God's advice, yet we don't listen to it. Prayer is a valuable asset in a Christian's life, but listening is essential if we want answers. Prayer and listening change lives.

Devote yourselves to prayer with an alert mind and a thankful heart.

Colossians 4:2 NLT

First pay attention to me, and then relax. Now you can take it easy—you're in good hands. Make insight your priority.

Proverbs 1:33 Message

Q. How can I demonstrate God's love?
A. God gave us this commandment: "You shall love your neighbor as yourself" (Mark 12:31 NKJV). In other words, you should show the same care and concern for the well-being of others as you do for yourself. We must be in touch with the needs of other people, and to do this, start with your own circle of friends. How can you love them through encouraging words and prayer? How can you be a blessing to someone else? Every single day you should make a conscious effort to be a positive encouragement in another person's life. Pick your victim today—it could be a teacher, parent, sales clerk, friend, sibling . . . most anyone welcomes a positive word or gesture.

Love other people as well as you do yourself. You can't go wrong when you love others. When you add up everything in the law code, the sum total is love.

Romans 13:9–10 Message

C4 Yourself

We all feel and experience different kinds of

Tammy's Tip

You can't do anything to make God love you. He just does. However, the choice is yours to receive it or reject it.

Love vs. Infatuation

love. There's the kind of love that we love our dearest friends and family with, and the kind that we are called to love all of mankind with, and then there's puppy love that turns us on to the opposite sex. But Papa love, the kind that we receive from God the Father, is the truest, purest form of love we will ever know. We just have to allow ourselves to experience it. You are God's child, Daddy's little girl, and with this adoption comes an inheritance of eternal benefits. Throughout life you will experience the joy of love and the hurt of love lost, both of which will mature you and bring you to a deeper understanding of the one constant in your life—God's love for you. You are Daddy's little girl and he loves you no matter what. Even when you disobey him, he still loves you.

Go ahead, allow yourself to be loved and hugged right now by your heavenly Papa. Take a minute to bask in God's love.

Be TRUE to YOU—Allow
yourself to accept the fact
that God loves you.

Teaming Up

Going Out

"Going out" has a whole new meaning these days. It once meant you were actually going somewhere, as in going on a date, but now it means you have been paired up with a significant other, someone you deemed worthy and gave the exclusive right to call you his "girlfriend." This is when you take puppy love to the next level and commit to your infatuation. It's pledging your allegiance to someone without being physically attached . . . or at least that's how it should be. However, in many cases "going out" is code for "making out." When we agree to belong to someone else exclusively, we often treat it as fake marriage without the vows. Of course, sometimes we even throw them in—"*I promise to always love you . . . blah, blah, blah*,"—hoping a few words will justify our actions.

"Going out" changes your life in many ways, sometimes for the better but many times for the worse. You often put yourself in vulnerable situations that could have been avoided by thinking ahead. The sad thing is, you may not give it a second thought until it's too late, and then you stand back and wonder, "What happened?"

"Going out" has its perks and quirks, so do yourself a favor and review the pros and cons and set your standards before you rush into anything.

Once you've landed a significant other, you can easily start losing your own identity as you jump into your new relationship. You naturally start thinking about the other person and his likes, dislikes, expectations, and needs, and you often start conforming to what your boyfriend wants instead of what's best for you. In this chapter we're going to map out ways you can have a steady boyfriend without losing your identity, interests, and individual friendships to his ideas. Going out is a two-way street—don't end up going the wrong way down a one-way street.

1 + 1 = a Couple

When we declare our love and make it official, the previous guy/girl rules are exchanged for a new set of expectations. You no longer consider yourself as an individual but now consider yourself as part of a couple, which often really means you put yourself aside and consider him and him alone. Your time and space has been invaded by another individual who may knowingly or unknowingly put demands on you that aren't worth losing yourself over.

Get a Clue

"Going out" is kind of like a prototype marriage that requires your time and energy and somewhat changes your individuality. In fact, you can get so caught up in your new role that you forget who you are until a snubbed friend points out the change.

Probably one of the biggest mistakes girls make when they get a steady boyfriend is disregarding their relationships with girlfriends. It's like Mr. Main Squeeze comes along and all of a sudden you can't squeeze in time with your old friends. They fall to the wayside as you journey off with someone else, hoping they'll remain loyal while you're gone. But the fact is, it doesn't always work that way. I can't even count how many stories I've heard from girls just like you who were neglected by their very best friend when some sweet-talking guy came by and

Tammy's Tip

Don't allow your boyfriend to become your only friend.

swept her off her feet. Don't let this happen to you and your friends. Set aside time with your girlfriends: time to hang out, talk, plan for the future, reminisce over the past, and make new memories to share. And a word of advice: leave the boyfriend out of it. Girlfriends like to hear about your guy now and then, but they don't want conversation about him to totally monopolize their time with you. Remember to make time for your friends. Don't alienate them; they may be all you have left when you break up with the boyfriend and need a shoulder to cry on.

Simplify

Be yourself. Save time for you and your interests. Keep your individuality, because that's what makes you, you. Don't ignore your own likes and dislikes to accommodate someone else. I mean, sure, you don't want to be selfish, but you don't want to be stupid either. For example, I knew this girl who was really smart—in fact, she was among the top three of her class—but then she started dating Dan the "party man." Studying was the last thing on his mind. He never opened a book and was bored to tears when Mary Anne wanted to study. As a result, Mary Anne compromised her standards and studied less and partied more. It really went against her natural personality because she was quite introverted, and she lost the one shot she had at being valedictorian of her class when her Spanish grade dropped from an A to a B. Mary Anne gave up her hopes and dreams of being valedictorian for a guy who ended up dumping her anyway. If she had applied some of her smarts to the situation, she would have scheduled fun time with Dan and study time for Spanish so that when Dan said "adios," she would have at least still been at the head of her class. Don't let a guy overshadow you with his personality; it's not worth it. If he doesn't like you and your character traits and you can't be who you are around him, then he isn't the guy for you. A relationship should be based on give and take, with each of you considering the other's wishes. For example, you pick the movie one night and let him pick the movie the next, or you sit with him some days at lunch but on other days each sit with your own groups of friends. Don't get in the habit of being joined at the hip, and you won't suffer the consequences.

FYI

When you make a relationship official by going steady with that certain someone, you develop a closeness that wasn't there before you were classified as a couple. You'll find that you can more easily isolate yourselves from other people as you get to know each other better. But this is dangerous! Guys and girls are naturally physically attracted to one another, and when left alone you may start doing what comes naturally—start making out—and it doesn't always stop there.

Now, don't take what I'm saying the wrong way. Having a steady doesn't mean you're having sex; however, it does move you a step or maybe even a few steps closer. How do I know? Because I've been there. It's like when you have a "one and only" boyfriend, you're hands-off to everyone else but fair game to him and vice versa. According to the world's standard, a new set of rules applies which pretty much says that if you're *going out* you're also *going all the way.* Don't let this be typical of you. Protect yourself and the guy you're dating from being typical. Strive to be different from the world's standard in all that you do, including your relationships with the opposite sex. Stay committed to your future because, after all, you don't want to look back and be sorry that

Tammy's Tip

Don't allow your fixation with boys to come between you and your friends.

you already gave away a one-time-only, nonreturnable gift. Save your virginity for the man you marry.

What's It 2U?

Before you get too involved in a steady relationship, lay down some ground rules. For example, I know this girl who wants to save her first kiss for her wedding day, so she let her boyfriend know right up front about her standards and gave him the option to stick around or flee the scene. And guess what? He stuck around. He said he had never met a girl with such high standards and was intrigued by her tenacious spirit. I also know a guy who felt smothered in his relationship with his girlfriend, so he explained to her that he needed time alone with his friends. She was okay with it at first, but then she started feeling jealous and didn't want to share him and broke it off. And you know what? That's okay, because obviously they were not a good match. After all, that's what all of us, both male and female, truly dream of—the perfect match.

C4 Yourself

Going out doesn't mean the same thing to everybody, but for most it will conjure up thoughts of love, romance, and what's in it for me? Both guys and gals enter into relationships with their own preconceived ideas of what "going out" is all about, and when things don't turn out the way they had hoped, breakup is inevitable. That's why it is extremely important for you to protect yourself from getting hurt in the long run. Take a break from your steady now and then to maintain relationships with close friends because when you mutually break up, or get dumped, a close friend will stick with you in your

You don't have to be "going out" in order to make a boy a friend.

time of crisis. Above all, protect your purity. Guys will come and guys will go but the gift of your purity can't be given back like a class ring or bracelet. With purity, once it's over it's over . . . The end.

Steady Goes It

Life, to a certain extent, resembles one giant romance. It's kind of like "going out" with that special someone—one day you're lovin' life and the next day you're ready to end it. The difference however is, since you can't always fix problems in life with a simple "breakup," by separating yourself from your circumstances, you have to make an effort to work through your struggles, and when you do, you'll end up a stronger person for it. But here's the cool part: you don't have to do it alone; you can go it steady with God. God makes everything better. No foolin'. Even when you think things couldn't get any worse, God is with you every step of the way.

Going steady with God changes your life for the better. I can't explain just how much, because you have to experience it for yourself in order to truly realize the endless benefits associated with this romance. God is faithful and his promises are true. He will never leave you, and your vulnerability is surpassed by his love for you. He will not avoid you; in fact, even when you reject him and try to go it alone, he'll patiently await your return. God is more than your very best friend—he's the lover of your life.

Going steady with God will have its perks and quirks, but as you weigh the expectations you will find that the advantages you gain from your relationship with God far exceed the effort you put into it.

Going steady with God gives you a new title: C-H-R-I-S-T-I-A-N. And as a Christian you have certain benefits

● ●

Going with God keeps you steady throughout all of life.

and responsibilities that weren't part of your old way of living:

> As a Christian your number one **Commitment** is to God, and the second is to **Help** others **Realize** their need to **Invite** Jesus into their lives. **Salvation** supplies us with **Truth**, which **Inspires** us to **Accept** what we cannot change and **Navigate** the things we can.

The Trinity + 1 (You) = a Couple

Once you accept Christ into your life, your old way of thinking about life is exchanged for new ideas. You no longer live without hope because you have put your faith and trust in Jesus Christ. You belong to him and vice versa. Your identity has changed. You are no longer a loner but instead are coupled with Christ. Ultimately, you have what is known as the Trinity, three-in-one, living in you—God the Father, God the Son, and God the Holy Spirit. It may sound a bit confusing at first, but what you must understand is, Father, Son, and Holy Spirit are one and the same.

> To see me [Jesus] is to see the Father. . . . Don't you believe that I am in the Father and the Father is in me? The words that I speak to you aren't mere words. I don't just make them up on my own. The Father who resides in me crafts each word into a divine act. Believe me: I am in my Father and my Father is in me.
>
> John 14:9–11 Message

> So Jesus was baptized. And as soon as he came out of the water, the sky opened, and he saw the Spirit of God [Holy Spirit] coming down on him like a dove. Then a voice from heaven said, "This is my own dear Son, and I am pleased with him."
>
> Matthew 3:16–17 CEV

Then I [Jesus] will ask the Father to send you the Holy Spirit who
will help you and always be with you. The Spirit will show you
what is true.

John 14:16–17 CEV

Get a Life

As a Christian you have a new life, and with your new
life you have new perks that were not available before. You
have the constant companionship of Christ living in you. He
never takes a break or a day off; he's there intervening on
your behalf 24/7. Now, just for a moment, let's contemplate
what that means.

God the Father, God the Son (Jesus), and God the Holy
Spirit are three persons in one person. And the Bible says
that when you accept Jesus, the Holy Spirit dwells in you.
Since God the Father, God the Son, and God the Spirit are
one and the same (known as the Trinity), that means all three
in one are living in you. You house the love of the Father,
the hope of the Son, and the leading of the Holy Spirit all
under one roof.

Don't you know that your body is the temple of the Holy Spirit,
who lives in you and was given to you by God?

1 Corinthians 6:19 NLT

Understanding the makeup of the Trinity can be a little
confusing, so let me see if I can make it a bit clearer. Let's
think about our grandparents for a moment. Do you have a
grandma or grandpa who
adores you? Well, your
grandma is someone's
mother and someone's
daughter, just as your

Tammy's Tip

Think of it in terms of math:
with God the Father, God the
Son, and the Spirit of God living
in you, you are 1^3

grandpa is someone's father and someone else's son. Yet your grandma is one person, and your grandpa is one person. Get the picture?

Grandma/Mother/Daughter = 3 in 1
Grandpa/Father/Son = 3 in 1
God/Son/Spirit = 3 in 1

The Simple Truth

Like superheroes, we've been gifted with supernatural power through the Holy Spirit. We've been invaded by the Holy Ghost. We are supplied with an unimaginable amount of strength that can be tapped into for any and all situations with just a little faith. You, girlfriend, are not by yourself; you are going steady with the almighty God, which gives you the

Time Out
with Tammy

When you understand the power given to you through the Holy Spirit, life won't be quite as overwhelming. You can learn to draw upon the strength you have in him and through him. You never have to go it alone again.

One morning while sitting in homeroom I was called over the intercom to the vice principal's office. All the way to the office I wracked my brain trying to figure out what I was in trouble for, but nothing came to mind. Once I arrived at the v.p.'s office, he greeted me and then proceeded to introduce me to this totally cute guy sitting in his office. It was his son, who went to another school. He had come to our school that day with his dad to take the PSAT test being offered that afternoon. The vice principal asked that I chaperone Todd around until it was time for the test. Needless to say, I was thrilled to have the opportunity to be seen with the hot new guy that all the other girls wanted to know.

My morning classes and lunch flew by, and then it was time to meet in the library for the PSAT. The administrator went over the directions and then passed out the test. Todd, who was sitting at my table, leaned over and whispered, "Keep your paper open so I can see it, and I'll do the same for you." I responded with a nod but knew what he was suggesting wasn't right. About a half hour into upper hand in everything you encounter in life. You have the power through Christ living in you.

You + God the Father +
God the Son + God the Spirit = a winning combination

or, to simplify:
God + you = the majority (always!)

When you stand with God, your side outweighs that of your peers or anyone else standing against you. You are on a winning team, so don't try to play the game of life alone. Depend on your team for assistance. It doesn't matter whether you're facing a situation you caused yourself or one that was created for you; just pray and depend on God for help. He loves you and wants to help you do the right thing. He'll also comfort, protect, encourage, and guide you through every circumstance you face. To put it simply, God is amazing, and

the test he kicked me under the table to get my attention and then signaled for me to move my arm. I didn't want to cheat, but I slowly moved my arm anyway, not wanting to seem uncool to this very cool guy. However, I knew instantly in the pit of my stomach that what I was doing was wrong. The Holy Spirit was convicting me about my behavior, but I still didn't know how to handle the situation, so I quickly prayed for some help. Within seconds I got my answer, "Scoot your chair to the left and turn your paper to the left, and you will be out of legs' and eyes' reach." I could tell that Todd was mad, especially when he started clearing his throat trying to get my attention, but that eventually stopped when the test administrator asked him if he was okay. At the end of the test he didn't even speak to me; he just flew out of the library and back to his father's office. I never saw him again after that, but that was okay, because I decided I didn't want to date anyone I couldn't trust anyway . . . even if he was one of the cutest guys I'd ever laid eyes on.

The fact is, this was a tough choice to make, and I know I wouldn't have been able to make the right call without the Holy Spirit prompting me toward the right decision. You too have the Holy Spirit's power—use it to your advantage.

you'll be amazed at how he can change your life for the better if you just let him. On your own, life can seem impossible, but when you're teamed up with God, the opposite is true: all things become possible.

FYI

When you're going out with that special guy, you want to avoid losing your identity as an individual. However, when you pair up with God, you want to find your identity in him. Being known as a Christian can be awkward at times, when we feel like we're being scrutinized, but don't go incognita when put on the spot. Stand up for what you believe and who you believe in.

God is the steady you want to be identified with and the one you want to spend quality time alone with, getting to know him on a more intimate level. Only by developing your relationship with God will you start to understand the power you possess through knowing him. You have basically two ways to romance the relationship and put it into practice every day: reading the Bible and talking to God.

My challenge to you: take time out right now to get to know God better. Read the Bible for *only* 3 minutes and then pray for just a couple more. That's it, 5 minutes total! Now, imagine if I said you could only connect with your boyfriend for 5 minutes. How does that compare with time spent with God? Are you as eager to spend time with God as with a guy?

What's It 2U?

Being in a love relationship with God requires discipline on your part. It takes self-control to work him into every fiber of your being. It requires strength of mind to know him

● ● ● ● ● ● ● ● ● ● ● ● ● ●
Be TRUE to YOU—
Experience God in
exceptional ways.

better through Bible study, strength of communication to understand who he is through prayer, sensitivity to listen to his sometimes subtle prompting, and strength of will to do what he says. All of these disciplines are essential to knowing what God is capable of doing in your life. Aim to spend time alone with God every day so you can start experiencing the power of God in your life. Do this by reading the Bible, praying, and carefully listening to the gentle nudging of the Holy Spirit. Trust me, once you start integrating the characteristics of Christ into your life, you'll wonder how you ever got along without him.

> For I can do everything with the help of Christ who gives me the strength I need.
>
> Philippians 4:13 NLT

C4 Yourself

God is the one steady you can count on. He will never leave you or turn his back to you. His love and dependability are a constant in any believer's life. However, even though he has given you his all, the fact still remains that this is one romance that you must invest yourself into. You'll take away more than you put into it, and the more you put into it, the more you'll take away from it. But don't take my word for it, because no amount of explanation can compare to experiencing God for yourself.

When you align yourself with God you can always be sure that you have chosen the right side, because remember,

God + you = the majority in all situations

Tammy's Tip

Make it a priority to know, love, and depend on God every single day.

First Date

First-date jitters are the worst. The nervous excitement makes your head spin and your stomach squirm. It's like you want to go yet you don't, because you've never been out with this guy, so you don't know what to expect. You plot, you plan, and you ponder your every move, everything from what you'll wear to what you'll say to how you'll respond if he leans over to kiss you. You want everything to be just right, just the way you dreamed it would be—the ideal guy, the ultimate date, and the perfect match all rolled up into one blissful experience.

You want what you romanticized your first date to be, and you're not alone. We all do it. In fact, we idealize our first, second, third . . . and hundredth dates, hoping that each will surpass the last, exceeding our wildest expectations. We like to fantasize about happily-ever-after before we even get started, yet we have to begin somewhere. In this chapter we're going to answer the most pressing questions about first dates, and I'm not only talking about your first date ever but also referring to all your first dates with a new guy. We'll consider questions like, Who should you date and where should you go? What should you wear and how should you act? Should you kiss him and when? Would or wouldn't you date him again and why or why not? There's a lot to consider when you start playing the dating game, and to play strategically you must plan your every step and be aware of his. Like playing checkers, you need to contemplate your opponent's move before he makes it and know how to counteract it once he does. Checkers produces one winner and one loser, but if you play the dating game right, you both can end up as winners whether or not the date itself was successful.

I dreaded my first date like I dreaded a trip to the dentist. Sure, it was a different kind of fear, but it was nervous anxiety just the same. It was like facing a dental checkup. The checkup itself was really no big deal, but I dreaded the "what ifs" that came with it. "What if I have a cavity? What if I need a root canal? What if he uses the drill?" Dating's the same way. A date isn't that big a deal until our overactive imaginations put a nail-biting spin on it. "What if he doesn't like me? What if he stands me up? What if my parents embarrass me? What if I humiliate myself? What if, what if, what if?" Dating is filled with questions, so "what if" you read ahead for some answers?

Date Check

You need to consider many things before you head off on your first date. Dating is a big step in your life and needs to be carefully thought out ahead of time so that you will know how to respond to both the anticipated and the unexpected. Don't be caught off guard. This is something you want to go into with your eyes wide open from start to finish.

Dating tip numero uno is *know who you're dating*. You want to know as much as you can about your chosen date, even if it's a blind date. What do you know about this guy? Other than the fact that he's totally hot, who is he as a person? What do you know about his character? What are his likes and dislikes? What about his reputation? Who are his friends? What type of personality does he have? Are you attracted to him, or are you awestruck with who he is—I mean, do you like the guy for himself or do you like him because he's the quarterback of the football team? • • • • • • • • • • • • • •

First dates often determine if it will last or be your last.

Answering the following questions will help you know what to expect from your date before you go out:

1. Which personality type best describes him? (circle one)
   a. Outgoing / spontaneous / storyteller
   b. Bossy / driven / opinionated
   c. Easy going / laid back / agreeable
   d. Shy / scheduled / intellectual

Understanding a guy's personality will not only give you insight into who he is but also give you an idea of your compatibility. Now, I'm not saying that you must have everything in common in order to get along, because in reality opposites do attract. For the most part we are naturally drawn to our own personality weaknesses. So, for example, if you circled that your potential date best resembles (a) Outgoing / spontaneous / storyteller, then compare that to which choice best describes you. This will give you an idea of how he'll act on the date and how you might respond to him.

2. What are his likes?
Favorite class?   Favorite food?
Favorite color?   Favorite movie?
Favorite sport?   Favorite hobbies?

3. What are his dislikes?
Knowing a person's likes and dislikes will give you topics for discussion on your date and will also help you choose where to go and what to do if the choice is left up to you. For example, if you know he hates Chinese food and he asks you where you would prefer to eat, don't choose a Chinese joint. Or if you know he likes

golf, that will give you something to talk to him about.
Use the information you gather to your advantage.

4. What type of reputation does he have?
This is valuable information. What have you heard
about this guy? Not everything you hear will be true,
but if he has a bad reputation, you definitely want to
question it. For example, if the rumor is that this guy
can't keep his hands to himself on a date, then you
need to be aware of that so you don't put yourself in
a bad situation. Or maybe you've heard that he's involved with drugs, even though you haven't seen any
evidence of it yourself. My advice? Get to the truth of
the matter so that your reputation isn't scarred by his
poor character traits.

5. Who are his friends?
A person's friends reveal a lot about a person. Does he
hang with jocks, skaters, the chess club, band buddies?
What type of reputation do they have? Are they known
as partiers or churchgoers? Remember, a person is often
a reflection of the people he associates with.

6. Is he a Christian?
This is probably the toughest question to consider. Why?
Because if he is a Christian that's great, but if he's not
and you are, then you need to carefully think about
how a dating relationship could potentially affect you.
Remember, the Bible says to not be unequally hooked
up (2 Cor. 6:14–15), so before you get too involved,
consider the consequences. I'll be honest, I've dated
both Christians and
those I hoped would
become Christians,
and neither date was

Tammy's Tip

Always be yourself. Whether on
a date or hanging with friends,
let you be you.

necessarily better than the other—however, I did feel more comfortable with Christians, because I could be myself and express my faith without feeling weirded out over it.

Simplify

Okay, now that you've found out about the guy you've agreed to date, the next move is to find out where you are going and what you are doing on the date. This will help you know how to dress and what to expect before he arrives to meet your parents. (And yes, your date should always meet one or both of your parents before you go out.) You don't want the following to happen to you.

One evening my date arrived to meet my parents wearing a shirt and tie. I thought, *Wow, did he want to make a good impression or what?* Upon the introduction my mom asked him where we were going. I had assumed we'd go to the movies because he had asked me earlier in the week if there was anything I wanted to see, but the answer was quite the contrary. "We're going to my cousin's wedding," he said. What? I was caught way off guard. I wasn't dressed for such an occasion, nor was I prepared to meet his entire family on the first date. I remember hustling down the hall to my bedroom to make a quick change. But even though I had put on a more suitable outfit, I never did feel quite right with what I had changed into. I spent the whole evening feeling out of place as I assumed my role amongst his family as "Joe's new girlfriend." This was an awkward date. I wished I'd known ahead of time what I was in for before I'd accepted the invitation!

Know where you're going so you can dress appropriately. And by the way, dressing appropriately also means dressing with self-respect. Dress in the way you want to be thought of.

If you want to be thought of as a sex object, well, then dress provocatively. I guarantee you that if you dress sexy, that's all the guy will think about the whole entire evening—sex! He will spend the entire date wanting a piece of you rather than concentrating on getting to know you as a person. Think about how your outfit will affect your date. It's not fair of you to dress up as a little hot number and then expect him to remain calm, cool, and collected during the date. Guys are visually turned on, so what you're wearing will totally affect his ambitions towards you. He may very well think that if you're willing to bare it, you're willing to share it. Remember that there's a difference between like and lust. You may dress slightly sleazy because you think guys like it, but in reality it's not *like* they are feeling towards you, it's *lust*. Big difference. Don't confuse the two. Dress with class and you'll be treated with a higher standard of respect, so dress the way you want to be treated. It's that simple.

FYI

Not sure if you're ready to date yet? Well, here's some trouble-free dating advice that applies to both girls and guys: try group dates. Group dating takes the pressure off so that you can relax and have fun with the opposite sex without trying to meet any one person's expectations.

Group dating was my favorite form of dating. Here's how we did it. Usually five of us (stick with odd numbers to minimize pairing up), both girls and guys, would pile in a car and go bowling, roller skating, swimming, out to eat, to the movies, or whatever. No pressure involved. We could just let our hair down, be ourselves, and not worry whether or not someone was expecting a kiss at the end of the night.

Tammy's Tip

Dress so a guy focuses on getting to know you better, not your body.

What's It 2U?

First dates determine whether or not there will be a second, third, and fourth. They give you a clue if you are somewhat suited for one another or totally incompatible. All first dates present these questions: "If he asks me out again, will I accept or refuse? And if he doesn't, will I be relieved or in tears?" Sometimes we approach a date with the attitude, "This will probably be a one shot deal," and other times we go into a date thinking, "I know this one is going to be the first of many." But it's bizarre how things turn out, because many times the dates that I thought had potential were actually duds in disguise, and the others that I thought were one-hit-wonders turned out the best. In fact, my husband is a guy I viewed as having little to no potential. Hmmm . . . I guess I'd have to say I was wrong about that one!

Rate Your Date

So the dilemma remains: how will you figure out if you want to give the guy another chance or turn him loose? Below are a few questions that will help you answer.

1. When he asked you out, was he: _____
   a. polite
   b. desperate
   c. insistent
   d. arrogant
2. When it came to meeting my parents, he: _____
   a. volunteered without being asked
   b. willingly agreed when asked
   c. was highly reluctant
   d. flat-out refused

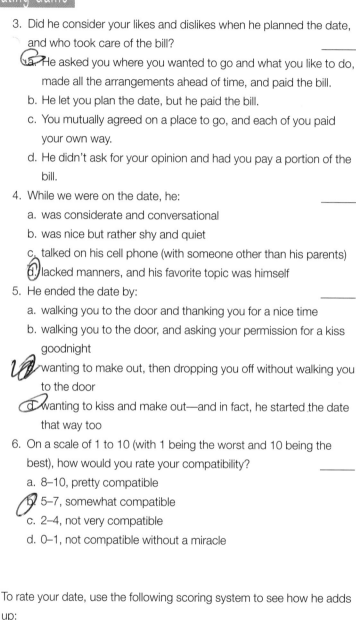

3. Did he consider your likes and dislikes when he planned the date, and who took care of the bill? _____
   a. He asked you where you wanted to go and what you like to do, made all the arrangements ahead of time, and paid the bill.
   b. He let you plan the date, but he paid the bill.
   c. You mutually agreed on a place to go, and each of you paid your own way.
   d. He didn't ask for your opinion and had you pay a portion of the bill.

4. While we were on the date, he: _____
   a. was considerate and conversational
   b. was nice but rather shy and quiet
   c. talked on his cell phone (with someone other than his parents)
   d. lacked manners, and his favorite topic was himself

5. He ended the date by: _____
   a. walking you to the door and thanking you for a nice time
   b. walking you to the door, and asking your permission for a kiss goodnight
   c. wanting to make out, then dropping you off without walking you to the door
   d. wanting to kiss and make out—and in fact, he started the date that way too

6. On a scale of 1 to 10 (with 1 being the worst and 10 being the best), how would you rate your compatibility? _____
   a. 8–10, pretty compatible
   b. 5–7, somewhat compatible
   c. 2–4, not very compatible
   d. 0–1, not compatible without a miracle

To rate your date, use the following scoring system to see how he adds up:

A = 3   B = 2   C = 1   D = 0

The Dating Game

Write each answer's number in the blank after each question and then subtotal your score.

Subtotal: _____

Next, check off all that apply from the list below. For each check mark, give him one bonus point.

( ) he's a Christian
( ) your parents liked him
( ) he was on time
( ) he opened doors for you
( ) he let you choose the music you listened to in the car
( ) he complimented you on what you were wearing
( ) he showed up with flowers and/or candy
( ) he took you home on time

First subtotal _____
Bonus points _____
Total _____

Scoring:

18–25 points: Ooh la la, this guy's a keeper. The fact that he excelled in so many areas means that he made his date with you a priority and went above and beyond the norm to get it right. If he asks you out again, say YES!

12–17 points: This guy has a lot of potential and deserves a second chance. He might not have been the most romantic, but he's far more sensitive than most. Although he didn't receive an A, that's okay, because B's are still above average.

6–11 points: This guy falls into the mediocre category. He wasn't the worst, but he was a far cry from the best. If I were you, I'd cut my losses and move on, but if you want to treat him as a charity case and grant him one more date, do it on your own terms and on your own turf.

0–5 points: Nope! This guy is a dope. Learn from your mistake and be glad you only had to date him once to find out he's not the one for you.

How did your date add up? Are you ready to go out again, or are you ready to bolt the opposite direction, hoping never to see the guy again? Still not sure? Ask your parents what they thought. Of course, if your parents are like mine, you won't have to ask; they'll just offer up their unsolicited opinions. In any case, make sure that no matter who you choose, you think it through and date smart.

C4 Yourself

Once you get a grip on how the whole dating thing works, your nerves will subside and the butterflies that felt like kickboxing elephants will settle down. You'll find yourself looking forward to some dates more than others and wishing that some would never end and others had never been. It's all part of growing up. And although you're bound to make mistakes along the way, yours can be minimal if you just follow a few simple guidelines:

1. Know your date.
2. Know where you're going, and make sure you tell your parents.
3. Know ahead of time what you'll say and how you'll respond if he makes unwelcome advances.
4. Dress appropriately—with respect for yourself and your date.
5. Carefully consider whether or not you want to date him

Tammy's Tip

Not sure if you're comfortable going out on a date? Then suggest dinner and a game or movie with your family. It might sound nerdy, but it's a good way to figure out whether or not he's worth the extra effort. (And, hey, it worked for me—this was my first date with the boy who became my husband!)

again if he asks, and if he doesn't ask, don't take it personally or make a big deal out of it. Keep your chin up and
confidently move on.

And don't forget, even though you can rate your date, dating can still be highly overrated. Give group dating a try, since
going out with friends lifts the pressures of dating one-on-one.
And remember, no matter what, whether you date one-on-
one or with a group, always date smart, because dating has
the potential to change your life for the better or worse.

First Love

As Christians we often get Jesus jitters. Sure, we love him,
but when it comes to making that evident in our lives, we
get squeamish. We think, "What will others think or say if I
talk about my faith? Will they tease or torture me
for it?" Many times we feel embarrassed about ac-
knowledging our love and acceptance of God. We
don't know how to tell the truth, so we often live
a lie to mask our identity in Christ. It's not that we
don't want to let our love be known; it's just that
we don't know what to expect if we do.

It's weird how things work. Even though we've
met the ultimate in God the Father, God the Son, and
God the Holy Spirit, we're still uncomfortable when
it comes to introducing him to others. We often even
think of various opportunities we have to witness,
but when it comes down to it we chicken out.

We fear rejection and long for acceptance. The
problem is, we've confused the two. We forget
where our acceptance and rejection come from:
acceptance from God and rejection from the
world.

You'll always remember your first date, so take the time to make it a fond memory.

The way you live your life comes down to being loyal and true to your first love. In this part of the chapter we're going to devise some ideas that will help you deepen your love for God and lessen your love for the world. After all, your goal should be to function without fitting in—or to put it another way, to live *in* the world but not *for* the world.

When we first become Christians, we're often gung-ho in our newfound faith, but once the newness subsides and we discover that it isn't as well-received by others as we had anticipated, we turn chicken and run to hide. We start thinking about all the "what ifs." "What if they make fun of me? What if they laugh at me? What if they won't be my friends?" We "what if" ourselves to the point of craziness, and from then on we're much more careful about what we say and how we say it. The last thing we want is to be associated with right-wing, wigged-out religious fanatics, right? So then we end up treating God more like a casual acquaintance than someone who loved us enough to save our lives. And why? There's only one reason: because testifying is terrifying. The fact is, we don't think we know how, so we just don't do it. And you know what? That's a lame excuse. I won't lie to you—being a witness is not easy. But it is possible.

Identity Check

If a casual friend had to describe you, how would they identify you? Could they ID you as a Christian by the way you act and the things you say? Would they have a clue that you know God, let alone love God?

Girl, it's time to do an identity check. Do you identify with Christ, or do you act more like those

Tammy's Tip

God is founder and overseer of the original witness protection program.

who don't know him? Do you love and follow the ways of the world, or do you love and follow God?

> Don't love the world's ways. Don't love the world's goods. Love of the world squeezes out love for the Father. Practically everything that goes on in the world—wanting your own way, wanting everything for yourself, wanting to appear important—has nothing to do with the Father. It just isolates you from him. The world and all its wanting, wanting, wanting is on the way out—but whoever does what God wants is set for eternity.
>
> 1 John 2:15–17 Message

Get a Life

Respect God. Put him first in your life. I don't know why this is so difficult, but I admit, it is. We can crowd God out with anything. Maybe you have a boyfriend, and the boyfriend

Time Out
with Tammy

I wish I would have figured out sooner than I did that my identity in Christ is the most important thing I have to live for. I could have saved myself a lot of grief if I would have made my top priority acting like a Christian rather than acting for the sake of a career in Hollywood. I wanted so desperately to please the world that I neglected God and hid my identity as a Christian just so I could fit in with the whole Hollywood persona.

This takes me back to when I was pursuing careers for myself and my young children (at the time) in television and movies. It all started when I was sitting around with the cast and crew on the set of the movie, *Calendar Girl*. It was lunch break and everyone was chatting over nothing in particular until the topic of religion was brought up; specifically, they were discussing how they were anti-religion, believed nothing, and thought that those who did were "brainwashed." I sat there quietly, trying to ignore the conversation—which worked until I was directly confronted about my opinion. I looked around, realizing that I was the minority, and half-heartedly shook my head in agreement with them. I had allowed peer pressure to sway my gets more attention than God, or you play a sport, and that sport occupies most of your time and energy. Or maybe you like to shop. Is getting to the mall more important than going to church? It's a fact: anything we devote ourselves to, other than God, can become our own type of idol. Now, I'm not saying that you need to cut these things out of your life, but I am saying that you need to prioritize, putting God at the top of your list. Know that God is a jealous God, and he wants and demands to be the most important part of your life.

One of the greatest distractions from God is the television set. It not only tunes God out but also tunes us in to the ways of the world. It takes subjects such as sex, drugs, and alcohol and turns wrongdoing into acceptable behavior. It burns away our conscious awareness of the things of God by making us callous to the sins of the world. Do your mind a favor: when questionable programming comes on, change the channel or turn the thing off. In fact, I challenge you to give up a half hour of television every day and focus on God. Use that 30

answer, and for what? These were people I hardly knew but was still eager to please. That day as I drove home I felt overwhelmed with grief, realizing that I had behaved like the disciple Peter, who had denied three times that he knew Christ (Matt. 26:69–75). Like Peter, I was afraid of what would happen to me if I told the truth, because I was out to win the world's favor, fame, and fortune. As a result I disowned God, pushing myself away from him. My lifestyle did not reflect who I was in Christ; it mirrored who I wanted to become in the world. And for this I have lingering regrets.

I wasted my time looking for happiness in all the wrong places. The place I needed to look was deep within my own heart and mind, the very place I'd buried Christ, trying to hide the fact that I knew him. Once I turned my life around and revealed what I had tried to conceal, I discovered for the first time ever the freedom of being myself and openly loving God. Making him your first love is the secret to a happy and fulfilled life.

minutes to read the Bible, pray, write in your prayer journal, listen to Christian music, or quietly reflect on your love for your heavenly Father.

The Simple Truth

Like I said before, it's not easy to stand up for the faith, but it gets easier each time you do it. After a while you will grow comfortable with who you are. You will naturally want and know how to uphold the faith when you're attacked by both the anticipated and the unexpected. However, in order for you to defend something, you must first know a bit about what you are defending. This is where the problem begins. We can't stand up for what we do not understand. Answering the following questions will help you know why you're a Christian and why you believe what you do. Then when others question your faith you'll be better prepared with answers.

What is the number one reason you became a Christian?

The number one reason I became a Christian is because I knew I had a *need* and that without having that need met through a personal relationship with Christ, I had no hope. Like the sick who are in need of a doctor (and sometimes don't even realize it), we are in need of the Great Physician who can save us from the penalty of our sin.

[Jesus] said to them, "Those who are well have no need of a physician, but those who are sick. . . . For I did not come to call the righteous, but sinners, to repentance."

Matthew 9:12–13 NKJV

Each of us has different reasons or circumstances that bring us to the saving knowledge of Jesus Christ. However, in any case the bottom line is our need. Everyone, no matter age, race, background, etc., needs a personal relationship with the Lord Jesus Christ. In him we find hope and without him all things in the end are hopeless.

Who is God?

God is our hope. He is the Creator, the giver and sustainer of life. **God is love!** And because of his great love for you and me, he provided eternal life for us by sacrificing the life of his one and only Son, Jesus.

> God is love. God showed how much he loved us by sending his only Son into the world so that we might have eternal life through him. This is real love. It is not that we loved God, but that he loved us and sent his Son as a sacrifice to take away our sins.
>
> 1 John 4:8–10 NLT

Who God is to me is who I've allowed him to become to me. When I was nine years old, I knew in my heart that I needed a change, but although I experienced salvation on the inside, I didn't allow the change to transform who I was on the outside. I welcomed God as my Savior, but I didn't take advantage of the power I possessed through him. God is all-powerful. God is to us who we let him be in our own individual lives. Those who exercise their faith in him more will experience him more.

The first step to testifying about Christ comes in the form of a lifestyle change.

Tammy's Tip

Prioritize and reorganize your schedule to not only include God but give him first place at the top of your list.

The Dating Game

Where is God in the midst of trouble?

He is right there in the midst of it. And although it may seem that he is distant, in reality he's right there waiting to be wanted. **God is everywhere, 24/7**, in the good times and the bad. But we usually don't call out to God when things are going well; we only call out to him when hard times hit. Sometimes I wonder, "Could it be that God allows bad stuff to happen so that we will look for him?"

I've been asked numerous times, "Where was God on September 11, 2001?" Well, based on the stories and stats I've read, I think God was busily at work saving lives. The fact is, 9/11 could have been much worse if God had not intervened. God was right there sparing tens of thousands of lives, and he's still right here today loving and encouraging those who lost loved ones because of this evil tragedy. God is always with you, both in the good times and in the bad.

How has believing in God changed your life?

God has promised me eternal life in heaven and given me hope while I'm here on earth. Because I believe in him, I have someone to turn to in all situations, both positive and negative, and when things get tough to handle, I have God to carry me through. **God is just a prayer away** from making a difference. Prayer changes things, and you'll never know how much until you try it for yourself.

The prayer of a righteous man is powerful and effective.

James 5:16 NIV

How can I begin to explain the changes for the better that God has brought into my life? It's one of those things I could brag on and on about, but you won't understand a word of what I'm saying unless you experience God for yourself. Every single day God changes my life for the better as my love for him grows deeper.

When your faith is being challenged, what should you do?

Short and simple: 1) don't deny it, 2) live it, and 3) be ready with an answer.

> Be pleasant and hold their interest when you speak the message. Choose your words carefully and be ready to give answers to anyone who asks questions.
>
> Colossians 4:6 CEV

When someone asks about your beliefs, be ready to answer. You'll always run into those who will try to put your knowledge to the test just to see if they can trip you up. Be on your toes without being defensive; know what you believe and why you believe it. Equip yourself with a short, to the point, sincere response that will make others consider what you have and who you are in Christ.

Why should my love for God be number one in my life?

God directs us to love him with all our heart (emotions), soul (spirit), mind (intellect), and strength (physical being). First and foremost, you are to love God completely. He wants every part of you. And it's amazing how your love for God will change you from the inside out. As it deepens it will help you become emotionally secure, spiritually awakened, mentally equipped, and physically able to be all that he's called you to be.

Why should we love God the most? Because according to the Bible, this is God's first and most important commandment for us to follow (Mark 12:29–30).

FYI

Telling others about Jesus can be soooooo painful that even those who are typically extroverts clam up when they have an opportunity to talk about God. Witnessing ranks right up there with anxiously awaiting a root canal. The sheer terror of it can make you sick to your stomach. It's panic city until the dentist comes in, reassures you, and gets you ready for the main event. He prepares your mouth ahead of time with a little novocaine so that the actual procedure doesn't hurt a bit. All you have to endure is the initial prick, and the rest is easy.

This is how it is with witnessing too. The unknowns of witnessing can make you feel nauseous just by thinking about it. Like with dental work, preparation is the key: know what to say before you say it. Prepare yourself ahead of time so that the only twinge you feel is the awkwardness of getting started, and then once you do it will get easier.

Not sure how to prepare your testimony? Please use the statement below to help you get started. Finish this thought either in the space provided or in your journal.

Knowing God has changed my life from the inside out by . . .

_____

_____

_____

_____

_____

_____

The Dating Game

What's It 2U?

Your love for God will determine how you live your life. Is he your primary motivation for living? How does knowing him and loving him affect the things you do and say? Is there a difference in you, or have you stayed the same? You won't change into Super Christian overnight, but you should slowly and steadily start modeling godly characteristics as your faith grows and matures.

Below are some questions to answer that will help you think about where you are and where you want to be in your faith.

Rate Your State

1. When faced with tough circumstances, the first thing I do is: _____
   a. pray for wisdom
   b. ask myself *WWJD?*
   c. call my friends and vent
   d. have a pity party for myself

2. During the course of twenty-four hours, I: _____
   a. pray more than 5 times
   b. pray 2–3 times
   c. pray if I remember
   d. pray only if there is an emergency

3. I read my Bible: _____
   a. every day
   b. 2–3 times a week
   c. once a week, on Sunday
   d. hardly ever

4. My friends know I'm a Christian: _____
   a. by how I live my life
   b. because I told them so
   c. because I wear a cross necklace
   d. (Shhh . . . they don't know!)

5. I demonstrate my love for God by: _____
   a. trying to obey him
   b. going to church
   c. keeping it private
   d. I don't know
6. When was the last time you told God you love him? _____
   a. today
   b. yesterday
   c. on Sunday at church
   d. I can't remember

Use the following scoring to see how you add up:
A = 3   B = 2   C = 1   D = 0

Go back over each question and write the number for your answer in the blank, and then subtotal your score.

Subtotal _____

Next look below and check off all that apply. For each check mark, give yourself one bonus point.
   ( ) you've shared your faith with someone at least once in the past month
   ( ) you've served in one way or another at church recently
   ( ) you've sent a thank-you note to your youth leader
   ( ) you've memorized at least one Bible verse in the past year
   ( ) you've written in your prayer diary/journal this week
   ( ) you've gone to church twice in the last month without arguing with your mom, dad, or siblings on the way
   ( ) you've read the Bible at least four times this week

First subtotal _____
Bonus points _____
         Total _____

Scoring:

18–25 points: Yeah! You are motivated by your love for God. Keep it up!

12–17 points: Stick with it. Don't lose sight of the goal, which is to love God to the best of your ability. Go back, look at the questions again, and identify the areas you need to work on. Then make those a priority this week.

6–11 points: Glad to see you're at least making an effort, but don't settle for average. Learn to love, serve, honor, obey, and praise God above and beyond the norm. Remember, God's Word says that he'd rather that we be hot for him or cold towards him—but not somewhere in the middle (Rev. 3:16).

0–5 points: Hmmm . . . looks like you need to straighten out your priorities. Add God to your to-do list and start living to love him today. Trust me, you'll be glad you did. I've yet to talk to one person who was unhappy with the results.

C4 Yourself

Our first encounter with God's love happens when we receive his Son, but that's only the start of experiencing God. Not until we return his love do we receive it back in its fullest form. Life becomes its best when you make God your number one priority and first love. This love will change who you are from the inside out and will enable you to stand firm in the faith even when others try to knock it down. Tell God you love him every single day and mean it with all you do and say.

● ●

Be TRUE to YOU—Always
remember your first love.

Dating Dilemmas

Do's and Don'ts

Dating can be mind-boggling. Should you or shouldn't you, will he or won't he, why or why not, yes or no, how and why . . . the dilemmas seem endless. Before you agreed to a date, the only thing you were worried about was getting asked out, but once you say yes, that's when the real worries begin. You begin weighing the do's and don'ts of dating and wonder if you'll know enough to get them right.

Advance preparation is key. It will help you avoid the pitfalls of dating. Knowing what to do and what not to do before you do something you shouldn't or don't do something you should is important to the outcome of your date. Some things you'll naturally think of, like planning your wardrobe, and others are less obvious, such as knowing how to keep yourself safe. Don't go into a date clueless but be clued into everything you need to know in order to get the most out of it.

I won't try to lie to you: no matter how much you prepare, dating is still somewhat nerve-wracking. But with a little advance preparation, you can be less stressed than most. So get ready for the in's and out's and do's and don'ts that apply to both him and her when going out.

• • • • • • • • • • • • • • •

When it comes to dating, take the lead by expecting the unexpected, and avoid being disappointed by keeping your expectations realistic.

Matter of Fact

Getting yourself ready for a date, both physically and mentally, is the first step to relaxing and having a good time. Once you've pulled yourself together, you will be able to approach the date with confidence, putting unnecessary fears to rest, which will make both you and your date more comfortable. Dating includes right ways to behave and wrong ways to respond for both guys and girls. Times have changed and so have the rules, but one thing has not, and that's wanting to feel extra special on your date.

Get a Clue

The first step to feeling good is to give yourself the special treatment before your date. Pamper yourself before you go out by taking extra time to get ready. As we talked about earlier, plan ahead of time what you're going to wear based on where you're going to go. And if it happens to be a surprise, ask your date how you should dress for the occasion and then get yourself together.

First things first: clean yourself up. Bask in a steamy shower using a fragrant shower gel or soak in a hot tub scented with aromatic bath salts—both are a great alternative to wearing perfumes, because you never know, your date might be allergic to fragrances. However, if you do opt for perfume, by all means don't overdo it. One more thing: while you're in the tub or shower, don't forget to shave your legs and armpits.

Once you get out of the tub or shower, pay close attention to both your toenails and your fingernails. Use a wooden orange stick to push your cuticles back while they are still moist. Next apply a base coat of nail polish and a quick-drying topcoat. Allow your nails to dry about 20 minutes before you continue to get ready.

Once your nails are dry, brush your teeth, apply your makeup, style your hair, and get dressed. Before your date picks you up, pack your purse with lip

Tammy's Tip

Use peppermint foot creams to keep your feet fresh and your shoes odor free.

gloss, mints, and those just-in-case-of-emergency items like a pad or tampon. Always take a cell phone that is fully charged and some cash for any unexpected crisis such as your date turning out to be a jerk. I know that's not a pleasant thought, but it's definitely one that needs to be addressed nevertheless. Once your date arrives, introduce him to at least one of your parents and make sure that one or both know where you are going and what time to expect you home.

Special note: Don't lie to your parents about where you are going or what you are doing. If your plans don't meet with your parents' approval, then change your plans, not your story. It's important for safety's sake that you always play it honest with yourself, your parents, and your date and that your date be truthful too. If your date is dishonest with your parents, he'll lie about other things as well.

Simplify

Once you're out the door and on your way, some more should's and shouldn'ts apply to both sexes. Remember, it's not cool for either party to overlook basic etiquette. Poor manners are never in style and can often make or break a date. Read on and you will find a list of do's and don'ts. Some apply to him, others to her, some to both, and all to the successful outcome of the date.

Now, I realize that you're not going to carry out the guy advice. However, knowing the do's and don'ts that apply to guys will give you a clue as to whether or not your date is worth the effort. For example, if your date gets off work from McDonald's and doesn't detour to the shower before he picks you up, that shows a real lack of consideration on his part. Quite frankly, if he didn't take time to fumigate the French fry smell, that would cause me to question his personal hygiene and would make me feel a little less special since apparently our date didn't merit cleanliness on his part. Remember as you're putting your best foot forward that you deserve someone who's going to do his best for you in return.

DATING DO'S

FOR GIRLS:

Do go on your date well groomed.

Do dress appropriately for your date. Wear modest clothing.

Do take a fully charged cell phone and money with you for emergencies.

Do tell at least one parent where you are going.

Do make decisions if he asks you to choose. Guys like it when a girl will step up to the plate and make a choice, not leaving everything up to him.

Do talk about things he is interested in.

Do unlock his car door if your date is courteous enough to walk around and open your door for you.

FOR GUYS:

Do show up freshly showered and neatly groomed.

Do show up with the car clean, inside and out.

Do open doors for your date.

Do pull out chairs for your date.

Do take her to a place where she will be comfortable.

Do bring emergency money just in case she was supposed to pay and doesn't.

Do be considerate. For example, if your date is cold, offer her your jacket.

Do call her after the date if you told her you would.

Do walk on the outside of the sidewalk and take the lead going down flights of stairs as a courteous way of protecting your date and keeping her safe.

FOR BOTH:

Do practice good manners.

Do be on time.

Do be honest.

Do be yourself.

Do be a good listener.

Do be considerate with the type of music you listen to in the car.

Do talk about each other's interests, not just your own.

Do find common interests and talk about those.

Do smile and compliment your date.

Do pay the bill and the tips if you were the one who did the asking out. (Did you hear that, girls? If you do the asking, you do all the paying.)

Do thank your date verbally for going out with you.

Do obey your curfews.

DATING DON'TS

FOR GIRLS:

Don't whine or complain to your date or the restaurant server. This could embarrass your date.

Don't order the most expensive thing on the menu, unless you're paying. A good rule of thumb is to find out what he is ordering and then order something that costs the same price as his meal or less.

Don't talk about your ex-boyfriend or compare your date to other guys.

Don't compete with him or point out his faults.

Don't mess with your hair in public.

Don't put down his car. A guy takes pride in his wheels.

Don't ask him to take you shopping or to sit outside the dressing room while you try on clothes, and absolutely do not ask him to pay for your stuff.

FOR GUYS:

Don't use coupons for dinner.

Don't walk out of a restaurant without paying the bill. This is a total embarrassment to your date, especially if you're caught.

Don't compare her to your ex-girlfriend.

Don't belch, pass gas, or scratch yourself openly in public.

Don't take advantage of your date.

Don't kiss her good-bye without her permission.

Don't expect sexual activity of any kind in return for the date.

FOR BOTH:

Don't be late.

Don't pretend do be something you're not.

Don't talk about your ex's.

Don't order foods that are awkward to eat such as spaghetti, ribs, or chicken on the bone.

Don't interrupt your date when he or she is talking.

Don't tell off-color jokes or use vulgar language.

Don't drink alcohol or use drugs. The moment he or she brings out drugs or alcohol,

Tammy's Tip

Being on your best dating behavior will produce the best dating results.

end the date right then and there. Girls, if he won't take you home, do the responsible thing and use your cell phone to call for help.

Don't talk nonstop about yourself.

Don't call or email repeatedly after the date. If he or she doesn't reply after a couple of attempts, leave it alone; it's probably a sign that it's over.

Don't talk on your cell phone while you're on a date, unless a parent or guardian calls—and then it's a must.

Don't treat your date second-rate, even if you already know there's no chance of a second date.

Follow these general guidelines and your date will be the best that it can be.

FYI

Does dating sound complicated? Too many rules and regulations? Well, I know one sure way to ease the anxiety of dating so you can relax and have fun. The answer is found in an "undate." The "undate" is sort of like a real date without any strings attached. An undate is when you jointly agree to go out as friends, pay your own way, and get your own transportation to and from the mutually agreed-upon destination. Undating relieves the pressure that real dating creates by equally dividing the responsibility between the two of you so that neither carries the exclusive responsibility of planning and executing the date. The burden of expectation is diminished and the excitement is intensified when the undate turns into a successful ongoing relationship.

Ready to give undating a try? Here are three easy ideas to get you started:

#1—Meet for coffee. It's easy, affordable, and quick. After just one cup you can decide if you're ready to take this relationship to the next level and meet for lunch.

#2—Meet for lunch. Once again, lunch is less of an obligation than dinner, and it usually doesn't cost as much either.

#3—How about a museum? Visit exhibits that each of you are interested in. This will give you topics for conversation and insight into each other's likes and dislikes within a public atmosphere.

Heed this undate advice: no matter how little it costs, pay your own way to avoid investing too much of yourself into a relationship before you're ready. And be careful where you go on your undate. You should always get together in a public place to avoid compromising situations; however, bear in mind that if you're out and someone else (like from school) sees you together, the rumors are likely to fly. "Guess who's going out?" "Did you know so and so were dating?" But be cool and don't let what others are saying ruin a good undating thing.

What's It 2U?

Dating is all about you and who your date is in relationship to you, not who you are in relationship to your date. What I mean by that is, watch out for yourself first, keeping what you do and how you respond in check with what's right, and then compare this to how your date measures up to your own personal comfort level. Once the date is over, carefully consider how you were af-

Tammy's Tip

Don't be afraid to ask a guy out on an undate or suggest an undate if he asks you out. Guys will normally welcome the idea because, after all, it lightens their responsibility and saves them money.

fected by the do's and don'ts in the guys' list. Did he observe common courtesies on your behalf? Now, he likely didn't practice every single one to perfection, but did he show you basic thoughtfulness, using basic everyday etiquette? There's no excuse for bad manners, especially on a date or an undate. Girl, you deserve the best. Don't settle for a second-rate date. You don't have to go first class in order to be given first-class treatment. It doesn't matter if you go out for steak and lobster or head over to the Golden Arches for a burger and fries—you can still be made to feel like a million bucks just by a guy's genuine attentiveness.

Take into account that some dates will be better than others, but when you follow the do's and don'ts of dating, the odds of having a good date are improved just by the fact you've put thought into making the date a success. My advice: make the best of it and hope your date does the same. And if he doesn't, there's one more don't to apply: **Don't** go out with him again.

C4 Yourself

Dating is risky business. It shouldn't be taken lightly. There are definitely right ways and wrong ways to date, and you don't want to be on the receiving end of a bad date. Lessen the stress by learning the basic do's and don'ts of dating, applying good manners, and always playing it safe by planning for unexpected emergencies. And of course, if it's simplicity and fun without commitment you're looking for, give undating a try. Remember, a large majority of the date is what you make it, so why not do your best to make it fun from the moment you agree to go out? No matter whether you agree to get together as a couple, as a couple of friends, or even as part of a group, make it a priority to relax, enjoy, be yourself, and have fun.

Pros and Cons

As a Christian, have you ever felt alone and strangely confused about knowing right from wrong? Has a hint of doubt ever entered your mind, causing you to question Christianity or perhaps wonder if it's really all it's cracked up to be and worth the effort? Do you find yourself thinking, *Gosh, if I wasn't a Christian, life would be so much easier and a lot more fun.* Well, relax, you're not alone. Everyone has had thoughts like these. I'm sure even Mother Teresa questioned the calling on her life a time or two.

The fact is, we're human, and as mortal beings we optimistically hope and pessimistically doubt all the time. We put our faith in God, optimistic that against all odds we truly have hope in Christ, but then our humanness interferes, contradicting our hope with a sense of pessimism. All of a sudden we question our faith and feel somewhat hopeless as we weigh the pros and cons of Christianity. We become slaves to do's and don'ts instead of servants of Jesus Christ.

Girlfriend, this section is dedicated to making you feel more successful and less like a failure in your relationship with God. It's all about God the Father's love for you and your love for him. My prayer for you right now is that you'll meditate on what you're about to read so that you can get rid of your guilt and walk away from this chapter feeling like the conqueror God created you to be instead of the failure Satan wants you to think you are.

As I was growing up, I never quite understood God's grace. My perception of God was that he was sitting on his throne just waiting for me to mess up so that he could judge and condemn me for my actions. I didn't comprehend anything about love, either God's love for me or how

Tammy's Tip

God doesn't want to make you a prisoner; he wants to bail you out.

Dating Dilemmas

I should love him. I was constantly trying to live according to a list of do's and don'ts, losing all sight of what it truly means to

> The do's and don'ts of dating will help when applied and hinder when denied.

be a Christian. To me Christianity was nothing more than a sort of imprisonment rather than freedom from the penalty of sin. I literally felt like I couldn't have any fun, like I was grounded for life instead of grounded in eternal life. I viewed God as a giant kill-joy instead of the joy of my life. The truth is, I just didn't understand spiritual matters and needed some God-guidance.

Matter of Fact

Once you became a Christian you may have become obsessed with rules—do's and don'ts that seem to rob you of your fun. The things you once enjoyed now riddle you with guilt, making you uncomfortable in your old surroundings. And instead of appreciating your conscience, you find yourself getting irritated with the results of your faith. I'm sure you don't like to stand out among your peers as the goody-goody, so perhaps you walk the fence, trying to live two different lifestyles, one accepted by your friends and one approved by God. It's like there's a war raging within you, one side pitted against the other, leaving you to make the final decision. The question is, how?

Get a Life

Whoever said "being a Christian is easy" lied. Living out your faith is hard work. The old you is drawn to what the world has to offer, but the new you desires to be more Christ-like. The two direct opposites leave you feeling split down the middle. You're faced with choices, right or wrong and good or bad, and they'll each have positive or negative effects on what you are becoming from the inside out.

> The old sinful nature loves to do evil, which is just opposite from what the Holy Spirit wants. And the Spirit gives us desires that are opposite from what the sinful nature desires. These two forces are constantly fighting each other, and your choices are never free from this conflict.
>
> Galatians 5:17 NLT

Have you ever seen a cartoon where a girl is perplexed over making a decision while a little angel (complete with halo) is perched on one shoulder encouraging her to do the right thing and a little devil is sitting on the other shoulder enticing her to make the worst possible choice? It's war between good and evil, and you're caught right smack-dab in the middle trying to weigh the evidence (pros and cons) each side presents. Both have valid points, and neither backs down as you twist, turn, and squirm coming to a verdict . . . and the decision is? Although I'm referring to a cartoon, that's how it is in real life. We have choices to make every single day, and most choices are either for good or bad. We can either choose according to what God would have us to do or what Satan would rather we do.

The Simple Truth

Once we start to appreciate the advantages of Christianity (other than heaven!), we start to take it less for granted and more seriously. Rights and wrongs no longer plague us, but instead we're able to argue the facts of why what's right is right, why what's wrong is wrong, and why what doesn't matter shouldn't matter. Let's look at some of the advantages that come with our faith.

Tammy's Tip

The number one benefit of being a Christian is that you are accepted by God.

To win you must believe you are a winner.

Dating Dilemmas

Advantage # 1: I'm a PRINCESS with a birthright

The number one benefit of being a Christian is that you are a princess, a daughter of the King of Kings and Lord of Lords.

> I will be your Father, and you will be my sons and daughters, says the Lord Almighty.
>
> 2 Corinthians 6:18 NLT

Birthright brings identity, and identity brings responsibility. Think of it this way. Prince William is destined to become the King of England, and with that position comes accountability. He has to answer for his behavior as part of the royal family. Our heredity in Christ is basically the same deal. Being a

Time Out
with Tammy

Should I or shouldn't I? If I don't I'll be sorry and if I do I'll regret it. If I go I'll wish I hadn't, and if I don't I'll wish I had. I want to, but I know I shouldn't, and if I wasn't a Christian there'd be no reason I wouldn't. . . . My brain was fried as I tossed and turned over going to my first ever party (with alcoholic beverages). I planned, I unplanned, I justified, I unjustified, I went from guilty to guilt-free, and then I finally decided to . . . go for it, with the stipulation that I'd bring my own Dr Pepper to drink.

When I arrived at the party, I was totally thrilled that I had decided to go because everybody who was anybody in two school districts was there. Needless to say, I was feeling totally cool to be part of one of the most happening parties that had ever taken place in the county. I walked around talking to everyone, sipping my soda, when all of a sudden one of the hottest guys around said, "Hey, Tammy, put your Dr Pepper down and come over here for a minute." I couldn't believe it. This guy had never talked to me before, and now he was calling me over like we were old friends. Of course I set my soda down and rushed over, only to be asked a stupid (drunken) question. "Do you brush your tongue when you brush your teeth?" "Huh? Do I what?" And then he started laughing his head off and said, "Never mind, forget it." I turned around, feeling embarrassed, grabbed my can of soda, took a sip, and made a quick exit. I knew instantly that the Dr Pepper didn't taste right,

princess makes you responsible and accountable to the King of
Kings and Lord of Lords. Your identity and reputation should
be based on who you are in relationship to him.

Advantage # 2: My PLEDGE of salvation is secure in Christ

The second great thing about being a Christian is that your
security is guaranteed. You have God's pledge of salvation,
and that cannot be taken away.

> Jesus replied . . . "My sheep recognize my voice; I know them,
> and they follow me. I give them eternal life, and they will never
> perish. No one will snatch them away from me, for my Father has

but everyone was laughing at me, so I decided to play along as they teased, "Hey,
is your Dr Pepper doctored up?" Yep, you guessed it, they had spiked my soda,
and within a few minutes my head was spinning and I could barely stand up.

I remember very little after that; in fact, about the only thing I do remember is
waking up on my girlfriend's sofa the next morning with a massive headache and
an extremely nauseous stomach. As I puked my guts out I started rethinking the
situation—wishing that I could go back in time and change my mind about going
to the party. I shouldn't have gone, and I was sorry I had. Justifying my actions had
left me riddled with guilt. The weird thing is, I had thought that if I went to the party
I would have a boost in popularity and feel better about who I was, but instead I
was teased all the more and ended up feeling worse about myself.

I know now that I made the choice I did because I was not comfortable with my
Christianity and felt insecure in my faith. I was just like the girl in the cartoon with
good telling me to do the right thing and evil suggesting I do the opposite. The
problem was, I felt constrained by rules and regulations instead of committed to
my relationship with God. One hurt and the other helped, and I didn't understand
it until I understood there were benefits and advantages to being a Christian. I did
what I did hoping for acceptance when in reality I was already accepted by the One
who really counts—God.

given them to me, and he is more powerful than anyone else. So
no one can take them from me. The Father and I are one."

John 10:25, 27–30 NLT

Salvation in Jesus Christ equals security for all eternity,
and that's exactly what you need to remember when Satan
tries to convince you otherwise.

Advantage # 3: I have acquired a new POSITION in Christ

The third advantage of being a Christian is that you are
literally a new person with a bright new future.

Since, then, we do not have the excuse of ignorance, everything—and I do mean everything—connected with that old way
of life has to go. It's rotten through and through. Get rid of it! And
then take on an entirely new way of life—a God-fashioned life, a
life renewed from the inside and working itself into your conduct
as God accurately reproduces his character in you.

Ephesians 4:22–24 Message

You are a renewed person with new hope. Your position
in life has changed now that you have entered into a relationship with Jesus Christ. You are no longer the old you.
You are slowly changing from the inside out as you develop
Christlike character out of your growing love for God.

Advantage # 4: God PROVIDES for me 24/7

The fourth benefit of being a Christian is that God cares
about you *all* the time. He gives you everything you need.

So whenever we are in need, we should come bravely before the
throne of our merciful God. There we will be treated with unde-
served kindness, and we will find help.

Hebrews 4:16 CEV

God is faithful. He never takes any time off from being your everything—your heavenly Father, friend, confidant, soul mate, helper, and everything else you need. He's there for you anytime, any place, for any reason.

Advantage # 5: God's PROMISES to me are faithful, true, and fail-proof

Without wavering, let us hold tightly to the hope we say we have, for God can be trusted to keep his promise.

Hebrews 10:23 NLT

God's promises are going to happen. What he says goes, and he never goes back on his word. That's the cool thing about God—he can be trusted 100 percent. He's not like any other friend you have, because he cannot and will not let you down.

Understanding the advantages of knowing God will help you grow to love him more. The more you love him, the more you'll respect him, and the more you respect him, the more you'll want to obey him. Think of it this way. You know how it is when you like that special guy—the more you like him, the more you try to please him with everything you say, do, wear, etc. Well, it's the same with God, except for one thing: he'll never walk out of your life. He's there to love and be loved 24/7.

FYI

Understanding your love for God changes the Bible from what seems to be a rulebook full of do's and don'ts and rules and regulations into God's love letter

Tammy's Tip

Anything worth having takes hard work and dedication—which means being the best Christian you can be is well worth your effort.

to you, which enables you to enjoy total fulfillment with your Main Man. Reading the Bible to find out how to love and serve God is a lot like perusing magazine articles on "How to Keep Your Hunk Happy." The big difference is that serving God leaves you happy, while the opposite is true with the boyfriend—you'll end up unhappy with yourself if you try to honor a guy's every wish just so he doesn't dump you. But God will never dump you, and he'll be thrilled by your attempts to please him.

The bottom line is, Christianity is all about one thing and one thing only, and that's *love*. The greatest part is that God loves you no matter what; the hard part is that we don't always love him the way we should by obeying him. It's our love for him that strengthens our faith and brings us into a closer relationship with God. In all of life the most important question you can ask yourself is, "Do I strive to love God the way I should?" "And you must love the Lord your God with all your heart, all your soul, all your mind, and all your strength" (Mark 12:30 NLT).

What's It 2U?

Has it ever seemed to you like the Bible was written to make your life less fun and more difficult? Have you ever read it and thought, *I could never be that good, so why even try?* Well, it's true, none of us can hope to measure up to the standard set by Jesus Christ, but we can try to move a bit closer to perfection every single day of our lives. As a Christian, you should pick up the Bible as an exciting source of support rather than a boring book of discouragement.

A couple summers ago I went hiking through the mountains with a group of high school students. The trails were clearly identified with arrows and signs that read, "To ensure safety, stay on the marked trails. Violators will be fined." Of course the guys in the group took this as a challenge and decided to sneak off and risk the consequences of blazing their own paths.

They thought they had gotten away with breaking the rules without anyone finding out—until a few hours later when they all ended up with poison oak. The rules of the trail were established to protect us from injury, not to steal our fun. That's how it is with the Word of God. It was given to us to help us, not harm us. God lovingly gives us guidelines to live by that are beneficial and liberating. Living life according to the Bible is all about freedom from consequences, not bondage to sin.

The Bible lays out tested and proven guidelines for better living in today's world. It is the number one best-selling self-help book ever written. Every single person who has read it and personally applied it has come out ahead. It's a fact: God's love never fails.

C4 Yourself

Loving God and understanding the advantages of loving him is key to making good choices, and the deeper the love, the better the decisions. When you apply this love you'll find out that the do's and don'ts of Christianity aren't so bad. They are simply 1) *do* love God with everything you've got, and 2) *don't* miss the opportunity to allow God to love you back.

Loving God and learning more about what you believe and why you believe it leads to a more confident relationship with Jesus. Your doubts about Christianity will lessen as your faith increases and you depend more and more on God. Not sure? Just try it. What do you have to lose? You'll never fully understand how much God loves you until you let him show you through prayer. You ask, and he'll answer. It's that simple.

The fact is, God is no party pooper but the abundant life of the party!

Be TRUE to YOU—Strive to live by the Word and for the Author.

Tammy's Tip

Try out the book of Proverbs for one month and see what happens. Read one chapter every day for 30 days and see if it makes any difference in your life.

Occasions

Prom Time

Special occasions require special planning. Unlike the normal date, special event dates involve advance preparation because they typically take more time and cost a lot more coin. I recently read that girls spent an average of $638 on the prom in 2002, and when you factor in that spending typically rises at a rate of 5 percent per year, the price of formal occasions just keeps on going up! Yet when you consider that you may be buying everything from a new dress to shoes, cosmetics, lingerie, and more, you can see how the budget gets eaten up much quicker than you might think.

Main event formals need out-of-the-ordinary attention to detail that rarely goes into planning routine dates. In this chapter I'm going to clue you in to how to make the most of your occasion with the least amount of effort possible. After all, special event dates shouldn't leave you frazzled with regrets but instead should leave you with positive memories that last a lifetime.

Have you ever wished that you could be like Cinderella and have your fairy godmother show up, wave her wand, utter a few magic words, and send you off with one simple warning, "It all ends at midnight"? That might sound good in theory, but there's something to be said for planning, because after all, planning your big event is half the fun.

Matter of Fact

Planning a formal is exciting, but it can also be exhausting if you don't know how to plan or what to plan for. You have to consider so many things before you attend an event of this magnitude, such as who to go with, how much to spend, your dress, hygiene, etiquette, after-event programs and parties, and the biggie . . . romance. Each and every one of these areas when carefully thought through will make or break an event. So, if you're ready, let's plan on making your main event the event of the year.

Get a Clue

First things first. Who are you going to spend the evening with? Are you going with a guy, a group of friends, or going it alone? The choice is yours. If you have your heart set on a particular guy, you might want to be the one who does the asking instead of waiting around. If he says yes, great, but if not, you need to make other plans. Remember, who you go with could make or break your evening, so choose the company you keep wisely.

Poise and Etiquette

Good manners are always in vogue, but in the case of a formal, they are expected more than in a usual setting.

Formal occasions call for out-of-the-ordinary formalities in order to make a typical date into an extraordinary event.

First, how is your posture? Do you stand and sit up straight? Not sure? Try this. Stand up straight and balance a hardcover book on your head. Now you are standing up straight! Practice walking and sitting up straight with a book on your head, and within no time you will improve your posture and appear to lose weight. Yep, that's right. Did you know that standing up straight can make you look up to ten pounds thinner?

Second, how are your table manners? Do you know how to use all those forks and when to place the napkin in your lap? Here are a few tips: Silverware is used from the outside in, with the exception of your dessert fork and butter knife. When you are finished eating, lay your silverware across your plate at the four o'clock position. This lets your server know that you are finished. And as far as the napkin goes, fold it in half or in a triangle and drape it across your lap as soon as you sit down. When you get up, lay it unfolded to the right of your dinner plate.

Romance vs. Sex

Something is enchanting about prom night. It's a special occasion with both guy and girl looking their finest and feeling their best. When you add it all up and throw in dinner and dancing, romance is naturally in the air. That's when it happens—you get caught up in the mood of the moment, and before you know it you're romantically involved and moving ahead sexually faster than you had anticipated.

Carlos and Tara hardly knew each other but mutually agreed to go to the prom together after a couple of friends talked them into it. The night of the prom Carlos looked hot in his tux and Tara looked gorgeous in her dress. There was a candlelit dinner, music, dancing, low lighting . . . what more was needed to set the mood? By the end of the night both were overcome with the events and romance of the evening, and Tara and Carlos were swept away by the moment. Shortly after the prom, in the back seat of a car, the night had a memorable end: it ended in sex. Tara lost her virginity, and later Carlos forfeited his soccer scholarship because Tara became pregnant. The two got married, had the baby, divorced a couple years later, and now regret the memory of their prom night.

The events of a formal occasion can often lead to sex, so many people say you should always go prepared. I agree. You should be prepared—prepared to deal with emotions, feelings, and events that you are not accustomed to. As you plan for your special event, don't forget to plan how to protect your purity. Learn the difference between true love and temporary infatuation. Guard your most valuable gift, the gift of your virginity, for the guy in the tux who anxiously awaits your arrival as you walk down the aisle dressed in a gown of white. Wait for the real major formal event of your lifetime . . . wait until your wedding day!

Outfit and Accessories

Finding the perfect dress, shoes, and accessories that fit you and the event may be your favorite part of a special occasion. We all want to look and feel our best without spending a fortune, and below are some ideas that will help you do just that.

- One of most girls' greatest fears when buying a dress is that they'll get to the event and see the same dress on someone else. This is easy to have happen considering that we all read the same magazines, peruse the same catalogs, and shop the same malls hoping for that one-of-a-kind find. Some stores keep a database of who bought what dress for which school dance to help keep duplication from happening; however, that system isn't foolproof since the same dress could be purchased elsewhere. Your greatest defense is to accessorize, accessorize, accessorize! Put your signature on the dress by personalizing your look with

Tammy's Tip

Save time and money by hosting a formal dinner party at home (with your parents' permission, of course) instead of going out. This way everyone can relax, have fun, freshen up, or actually wait to change into their formal attire until after dinner.

your own individual style. Accessorize with jewelry, gloves, wraps, brooches, bows, stockings, and so on.

- Shop vintage stores and thrift shops for that one-of-a-kind look that you won't find anywhere else. I have a gorgeous black skirt that I bought at a thrift shop for only $4.50! I've worn it several times with different inexpensive tops for new looks for just a few bucks. Remember, even if you find a dress that is too big, you can always take it to a tailor and probably have it altered for less than a new dress.

- My daughter and her group of friends would often swap formal dresses from one year to the next, adding new accessories to achieve a look of their own. And you know what? No one ever noticed that they were wearing each other's formals from prior years because each girl brought her own individual style to the outfit.

Makeup and Hair

The finishing touch is not complete until you have put on your makeup, polished your nails, and styled your hair. These are details that positively accent any outfit on any occasion. You can do it all at home or have it done professionally at a salon. With a little know-how, however, you can achieve the same great look at home that you get at the salon.

- Applying cosmetics is fun and easy and can look professionally done if you take your time, work in suitable lighting, and pay close attention to detail. Starting with a fresh, clean face, apply foundation that matches your skin tone, blending it evenly into your jaw line. Hide imperfections with a dab of concealer, blend your blush into the apples of your cheeks, apply eyeliner sparingly, and use shadows that compliment your eyes and

Extra! Extra! *Read All about It!*

For more help on fashion, hair, and makeup, read my books *Looking Good from the Inside Out* and *Looking Good from the Inside Out: Fashion*.

wardrobe. Follow up with mascara and a fabulous lip liner and color, and *voilà*! You're a work of art! Pack a translucent powder compact and lip color in your handbag and you'll be ready to touch up as needed. **Special note:** Also pack a band-aid in case of a broken nail, a safety pin in case something pops, breath mints, a cell phone, a little money, tampons or pads if needed, and a house key so you can let yourself in when you get home.

- Manicures and pedicures are a must when you're trying to look your very best. Nothing fancy is needed, just a couple coats of polish (that compliments your outfit) applied to your fingernails and toenails followed up with a fast-drying topcoat.

- Your hair is one of your most overlooked accessories. The longer your hair, the more options you have; however, short hair can be redefined too. Hair accessories are available in abundance and can jazz up an outfit as much as jewelry. Look through magazines for hairstyles to copy, and if you find one and are having your hair done professionally, be sure to take the magazine picture with you.

Simplify

You have to factor in so many things when planning major events such as homecoming or prom. Some are obvious and some not so obvious, but all are critical to the overall outcome of the occasion. To get a better idea

Tammy's Tip

You can create an up-do using one full can of extra-hold hairspray and at *least* one package of bobby pins. You'll need some practice, but with a little patience and a lot of time, you can save serious money by doing it at home.

of what I'm talking about, consider the following questions for starters.

What is the event?

The occasion will determine what you wear, possibly the flowers you choose, and whether you should go out to dinner first or a meal will be provided.

Who will you go with?

Who are you going with? Who will buy the tickets and pay for the photographs? Remember, the right or wrong date could make or break your special event.

When is it?

What time does the event start and end? This is important information to know because many high schools have adopted strict schedules that adhere to prompt arrival and departure times, and if you violate them, you can be left out. The other thing to consider when planning outfits and activities is the time of year—autumn, winter, spring, or summer—and the type of weather you can expect in that particular season.

Where is it?

Where is it and who will provide safe transportation?

How will the event unfold?

How is this thing going to happen? Are you going to dinner first? To after-parties later? And if so, should you wear your formal or change in between happenings?

You need to address all of these major questions as well as a few others which you will find in the following checklist.

FYI

We often overlook things for one simple reason—we're too busy! We tend to remember the major stuff, but the small things are often missed at the last minute because of our hectic schedules. Use the checklist below to help you plan ahead and take care of the minor details as well as the major necessities.

Event: _____

    Date of Event:_____

    Time of Event:_____

Name of your date/escort: _____

    Date you'll ask him if he hasn't asked you yet: _____

Who is buying the tickets? _____

    Have the tickets been purchased?   YES   NO

    Are pre- or post-event tickets (such as for an after-prom party) needed?   YES   NO

    Who is purchasing these tickets? _____

    Have they been purchased?   YES   NO

Who is paying for the photographs? _____

    How much are they? _____

    Are the photographs sold in sets (one for him and one for her) or are they sold individually? _____

    Do they need to be paid for in advance?   YES   NO

    If so, when is payment due? _____

Tammy's Tip

Do you sit dances out because you don't know how to dance? Try renting or buying a dance lessons video or DVD and learn how to dance in the privacy of your own home. It worked for me!

21

Have you acquired your dress and shoes? If so, does the dress need alterations, or do the shoes need to be color dyed to match the dress?

Dress: _____   Shoes: _____

Schedule dress and shoe alterations at least four weeks in advance (time frame may depend on your tailor and shoe shop).

Alteration drop off date: (dress) _____ (shoes) _____

Alteration pick-up date: (dress) _____ (shoes) _____

Does anything you will be wearing need to be dry-cleaned?   YES   NO

Dry-cleaning drop-off date: _____

Dry-cleaning pick-up date: _____

Will your escort be renting a tux and/or tux accessories to match your dress?   YES   NO

If so, give him a sample of the color to take with him. Hint: find a matching paint swatch at a home improvement store so he has something that's easy to carry with him in his wallet.

Have you acquired all the needed accessories for your outfit? Check off all that apply.

_____ Necklace   _____Earrings   _____Bracelet

_____Wrap / Jacket   _____Handbag   _____Gloves

_____Makeup   _____Breath Mints   _____Hair Accessories

_____Pantyhose   _____Special Lingerie (such as strapless bra)

_____Other: _____

Are you doing your own hair, nails, and makeup, or are you having them done? If you will have them done, book an appointment at least two months prior to the event.

Hair appointment   Date: _____   Time: _____
Location: _____

Makeup appointment   Date: _____   Time: _____
Location: _____

Manicure appointment   Date: _____   Time: _____
Location: _____

Special Occasions

Pedicure appointment   Date: _____   Time: _____

Location: _____

Are you going out to dinner first?   YES   NO

    Who is paying for dinner? _____

    Will you go in your formal attire, or will you eat first and then go back to your house to change clothes? (I recommend that if you are going to change clothes, you do it at your house because you will have a lot more stuff to transport than your gentleman escort.) _____

Will you be attending an after-event party of some sort?   YES   NO

    If so, what will you wear? _____

    If you are changing out of your formal clothes, bring a garment bag and small tote bag with you to transport your clothing, shoes, accessories, and personal hygiene items such as deodorant, toothpaste, toothbrush, hairbrush, and hairspray.

Have you ordered your date's boutonniere?   YES   NO

    What is the name of the florist? _____

    When is the scheduled pick-up? _____

    Hint: Be sure to let your date know ahead of time whether you would prefer a shoulder, wrist, or waist corsage. (This will also act as a subtle reminder to him to order the flowers.)

Who is providing safe and reliable transportation to and from the event?

_____

    Your safety is key in this situation. Have a backup plan just in case your date dabbles in drugs or alcohol. I was put in this situation myself, and trust me, you need a plan.

What's It 2U?

Most of your planning will probably be centered on getting ready for the main event; however, you

Tammy's Tip

Drinking and driving produce grave results. Statistics taken by MADD (Mothers Against Drunk Driving) indicate deaths due to alcohol-related automobile accidents rise dramatically around the times of prom and graduation.

need to plan for some other things as well. You need to strategize for situations we don't like to think about. For example, what do you do if your date doesn't dance? Do you a) find someone else to dance with, b) sit with your date, or c) dump your dud of a date and hang with your friends? The answer is, always practice common courtesy: a) it's okay to dance with someone else as long as you clear it with your date first; b) don't dance every dance with someone else, but instead take time to sit with your date as well so he doesn't feel left out; and c) never ditch your date and leave with your friends—unless, of course, your date is drinking, using drugs, or forcing himself on you. In that case, split the scene!

These are the kinds of circumstances you need to plan for—ones that are not exactly pleasant to think about but need to be addressed nonetheless. Below is a list of true-to-life scenarios and responses that a group of college freshmen shared with me. You may find several situations in which you could find yourself. Read each circumstance carefully and then circle the answer that best applies to how you would handle it.

What do you do if your date asks his old girlfriend to dance?

a. Go to the girls' bathroom and cry
b. Find your old boyfriend and ask him to dance
c. Keep a stiff upper lip and remember that he didn't ask her to marry him; he only asked her to dance

Although the first two responses might seem tempting, let's stick with C as the most correct reaction. Be cool about it, and after the dance calmly let him know how you feel.

Special Occasions

What do you do if you're feeling nervous about dancing, so your date offers you a beer to loosen you up a little bit?

  a. Decline

  b. Accept—after all, what can one beer hurt?

  c. Force yourself to dance the first dance, knowing that after you do, the following dances will get easier

The right answers are A and C; however, some might pick B thinking, "What can one beer hurt?" But what you may not realize is 1) underage drinking is illegal, and 2) once you have one beer, what's stopping you from guzzling the whole case? The truth is, before you have your first, it's easy to commit to the "just one" theory, but after "just one" your thinking is chemically altered, so you think, *why not two or three more?* Drinking and driving happens the same way. Anyone who is sober will say, "I'd never drink and drive," but alcohol impairs your thinking, and that's the reason we need organizations like SADD (Students Against Drunk Driving) and MADD (Mothers Against Drunk Driving). Think about it: better to be a little uptight and too nervous to dance than to be dead because you took your first drink.

How do you stop the mood when you and your date are both turned on sexually?

  a. Hit the cold showers

  b. Take control of your senses

  c. Do what you want as long as you don't go all the way

Although A and B are both the right answers, A is not necessarily very realistic under the circumstances. Answer B, however, is quite easy to do, and to do fast. The sooner you break the mood, the better, because after you let things go so far, it's almost impossible to stop, no matter how much you want to. One student's response was great. She said whenever she thinks about having sex, "I think of getting pregnant, having a baby, and dirty diapers, and that ends the mood."

The bottom line is, be ready for the unexpected. Think ahead. Make a plan before you have to. You're better off thinking through unpleasant possibilities ahead of time than living through them later on.

For example, I remember worrying about whether my date would kiss me and if he did, would he stick his tongue in my mouth? And that was only the beginning of my worries. What if he kisses me but it doesn't stop there and his hands start wandering into undisclosed places? What will I say? How will I stop him? These are all things you need to consider and plan ahead for if you choose to go out one on one. Be prepared with answers. Once a guy asked me if I wanted to get in the back seat of his car, and my reply was, "No, I'm fine. I'd rather sit up front with you." He looked at me like I was a total ditz, but he didn't ask me again. What will your response be if you're confronted with a handy date?

Be ready for whatever your date tries on you, whether it's kissing, petting, or sex. Decide now how far you'll go. However, I would suggest that you don't even put yourself into that situation but instead give group dating a try. Arrange group dates with some of your friends so you can focus on having fun and put all your anxieties to rest.

C4 Yourself

Formals are the kind of event dreams are made of. Our imaginations take us beyond reality to a magical place of perfectly met expectations. We hope and plan for the perfect date, dress, and night of dancing which will make the evening worth every single penny spent. After all, we want our money's worth and a whole lot more. However, the key to making positive memories is often found in what you make of the event. To help ensure your expectations are met, choose your date wisely, make a plan, schedule the details so that nothing is missed, and by all means, plan on making special memories!

Formals turn a date into a special event to be remembered.

Homecoming Time

Special occasions do require special planning, and each and every one of us is going to experience a certain main event in one way or another—and that celebrated happening is our homecoming. This is the appointed time when we will come face to face with Jesus Christ, either through our own death or the second coming of Christ. Many of us neglect to think about this time because we are all about the here and now and not about the there and later. We've got living to do today, not realizing that how and why we live now is preparing us for tomorrow, an eternity with Christ.

Your time on earth is advance preparation for things to come, but unlike the prom or some other formal event, this occasion has already been paid for at the ultimate price: it cost Jesus his life. Your homecoming has been paid for; the only thing you have to do is get ready.

Life is all about one of two things. If you have a personal relationship with God, it's all about serving him and getting to know him better before you go to heaven. If you don't know God, you may not realize it, but it's all about self-service and trying to make your heaven here on Earth before you spend an eternity in hell.

In this chapter we're going to get excited about the hope of heaven. Like a formal event that we plan and prepare

for, heaven's homecoming should be approached with great
anticipation.

Matter of Fact

As Christians we have something to live for that surpasses
anything else life has to offer, but we so easily forget about
eternity and lose sight of heaven as day-to-day living diverts
our attention. Shortsightedness is a bad habit we all fall into.
Have you ever heard the saying, "Hindsight is always 20/20"?
How true it is! If we could see the future, the decisions we
make and the things we do today would change drastically.
We would no longer think of heaven as a fairytale destination but as a place of promise for those who know and love
God on a personal level. We would make our homecoming
preparation a lifetime priority.

Get a Life

I've visited some mega-awesome places and have experienced
earthly beauty that has left me wondering how heaven could
possibly be any better. I remember staring out over the majestic
scenery of the Grand Canyon, trying to fathom that heaven's
glory will far surpass Earth's grandeur. I've seen much of God's
handiwork across the land in places like Yosemite, Yellowstone,
Niagara Falls, the beaches of Hawaii, and the glaciers of Alaska,
yet none of these compare to what we'll encounter once we pass
through those pearly gates and walk the streets of gold (see Rev.
21:21). Just imagine—the largest castles and the most luxurious
mansions here on earth will never measure up to what Jesus is
preparing for you in heaven.

In My Father's house are many
mansions; if it were not so, I

From birth on you're
homeward bound, and the
compass of your heart will
determine which way
you'll go.

would have told you. I go to prepare a place for you. And if I go
to prepare a place for you, I will come again and receive you to
Myself; that where I am, there you may be also.

John 14:2–3 NKJV

Wow! Just the thought of it sends shivers up and down
my spine. A mansion, with all the trimmings and trappings,
things many of us hope for but few have here on earth. I don't
know about you, but I believe God gave us a glimmer of what
heaven will be like in order to entice us with what's awaiting
us in heaven. God loves us and is preparing our homecoming
even now. Christian, this world is not your home, it's just a
temporary pit stop. It's like when you travel and stay in a hotel
temporarily. While you stay you enjoy the various comforts
the hotel has to offer such as television, cable, swimming
pool, sauna, and weight room, and then when your stay is
up, you leave behind what you borrowed and return home.
That's how it is here on earth—we're merely passing through,
enjoying the comforts of life God has seen fit to loan us until
we reach our heavenly home. So keep your focus upward
rather than outward, because what you treasure most will
be reflected in how you live your life.

Don't store up treasures here on earth, where they can be eaten
by moths and get rusty, and where thieves break in and steal.
Store up your treasures in heaven, where they will never become
moth-eaten or rusty and where they will be safe from thieves.
Wherever your treasure is, there your heart and thoughts will
also be.

Matthew 6:19–21 NLT

Christians are only pass-
ing through this world on
their way to heaven. Con-
sider this life a practice test.

Tammy's Tip

Whenever you're feeling down
in the dumps, turn your
attention upward to heaven.

Time on earth, with its tragedies, trials, and temptations, is preparing you for a triumphant life on the other side. It's to your benefit that you realize life here on earth is temporary. The good stuff is on the other side of death or Jesus's return, whichever comes first.

> There's far more here than meets the eye. The things we see now are here today, gone tomorrow. But the things we can't see now will last forever.
>
> 2 Corinthians 4:18 Message

The Simple Truth

It's time to do a reality check as far as your values, influence, and priorities are concerned. What does your standard of living say about you? Does it reflect the here and now, or does it reflect an eternity in heaven? To get a better idea of what I'm talking about, consider the VIPs of life.

Values

> It is not that we think we can do anything of lasting value by ourselves. Our only power and success come from God.
>
> 2 Corinthians 3:5 NLT

What do you value most in life and why?

_____

_____

Your spiritual values should outshine your worldly interests. Spiritual values are those things that draw us closer to God while worldly interests can do the exact opposite if we allow them to. For example, being part of a soccer team is an awesome experience. However, if you allow it to draw you away from Sunday worship at church it becomes a negative rather than a positive influence in your life. Not sure about your value system? Then ask yourself this question, "Do my values line up with those found in the Word of God?" This is what you have to determine every single day as you make choices that affect your future. Remember, the world and its belief system is on its way out, but God's standards will last forever.

Influence

My dear friends, don't let public opinion influence how you live out our glorious, Christ-originated faith.

James 2:1 Message

What or who has the biggest influence on your life and why? _____

You have the power to influence and be influenced for the good or the bad. The choice is yours. How will you affect those around you, and how do those around you affect your lifestyle? What do your standards say about your faith in God? Does your lifestyle represent the Word or the world? Remember, your influence could save a life from an eternity in hell.

Priorities

Your heavenly Father already knows all your needs, and he will give you all you need from day to day if you live for him and make the Kingdom of God your primary concern.

Matthew 6:32–33 NLT

Define a *need*: _____
Are any of your needs unmet?   YES   NO
    If so, what? _____
What is the difference between a need and a concern?

_____

> And my God will meet all your needs according to his glorious
> riches in Christ Jesus.
>
> Philippians 4:19 NIV

God has made your needs his number one concern, beginning with your need for a Savior. Your well-being is God's number one priority. It's not his faithfulness to you that is in question but your faithfulness to him. Is God your primary concern? Are your priorities all about loving and knowing him better or about loving yourself and making yourself more well known? Set your priorities according to God's plan and purpose, and your life will be fulfilling far beyond what you could ever imagine.

What do you value? Do your priorities reflect that? What type of impression does your lifestyle make? You are a VIP in God's eyes, and as a very important person, you need to value his standards, represent his influence, and make your homecoming a priority in life.

FYI

You should know that people of all ages and genders have difficulty with prioritizing. This is particularly tough for me. It's not that I don't want to prioritize; it's just that I get so caught up in day-to-day activities that I often forget what's most important.

God says that your number one concern should be your relationship with him and your second should be relationships with others. Let's take a look at your schedule and see if what's most important to God is most important to you too.

Start by making a list of your priorities, starting with the most important and working your way down the list. (Use a sheet of paper if you need more space.)

	Priority	Time spent on priority per day	Time spent per week
1.			
2.			
3.			
4.			
5.			
6.			
7.			
8.			
9.			
10.			

Priorities are a funny thing, because often our top priorities are not the ones we invest the most time and energy into. For example, let's say your list reads: 1) time with God, 2) time with family, 3) time with friends, 4) time with boyfriend, 5) television, etc. Now, when you compare your priorities from the greatest to the least important, does the time spent on each activity reflect the level of importance that you assigned each priority? The time will tell what is most important to you. Does your use of time reflect what is most important to you, or do you need to work on your schedule in order to make the two balance?

Remember this: when you make God your number one priority, everything else will fall into place.

What's It 2U?

Living with a "kingdom of God" perspective helps you stay focused on what's important. As Christians we are to direct our attention toward our heavenly home and treat this world as foreign soil. We are strangers merely passing through on our way to

Tammy's Tip

Time with God can save you in the end.

our homeland. We may feel like even though we speak the language, eat the food, and dress like the natives, an unsettled feeling still tugs at our souls and makes us eagerly await what God has in store for us when he welcomes us home. Wondering about eternity and what heaven will be like is normal. In fact, sometimes you'll find yourself thinking that heaven can wait, and other days you'll wonder how much longer you'll have to wait before you get there. Life is full of ups and downs, and our kingdom perspective keeps us on track, heading in the right direction without looking back.

> Don't shuffle along, eyes to the ground, absorbed with the things right in front of you. Look up, and be alert to what is going on around Christ—that's where the action is. See things from his perspective.
>
> Colossians 3:2 Message

How does a kingdom perspective affect your thinking? Does it impact your behavior at home or at school? Does it affect the way you approach a job or do your schoolwork? What about when you hang with your friends? Does focusing on a future in heaven motivate you to do the right thing when your friends are encouraging you to make poor choices?

Time Out
with Tammy

Schedules are an amazing thing. I don't know how they work, but it's miraculous to see them in action when God manages your time. Someone told me that if I made time with God my number one priority, I would always have time for everything else I needed to accomplish in a day. I thought, "No way." After all, when I tried to spend time with God before I went to bed, half the time I fell asleep from sheer exhaustion. So with a schedule like mine, how on earth could I possibly start my day with God and still get done everything I needed to do? The answer is, I don't know how it works, but it does. When you start your day with God, you'll find you don't lose time but gain it.

Take the "Make Time Challenge." For one week, start your day with God, and see for yourself how time with God adds to your day!

Your integrity is based on what you believe, and what you believe should be based on Christ.

C4 Yourself

Eternity is what our lives were made for. And although most of what heaven will be like is left to our imaginations, I can promise you this: it's worth the wait. Today, tomorrow, or eighty years from now, no matter how long the wait, it's worth living for.

Your life is a dress rehearsal for the main event; it's all about getting ready for your big homecoming. The question is, are you ready for opening night? Your life should reflect your future. It's like preparing for a career. No matter the occupation, it will require a certain amount of training or schooling to groom you for your future job. That's the way it is with life—it's all about getting ready and becoming more Christlike here so you'll be ready for your homecoming.

● ● ● ● ● ● ● ● ● ● ● ● ● ● ● ●
Be TRUE to YOU—Live for heavenly times ahead.

Tammy's Tip

When you set your sights on heaven your value system will reach a whole new level.

Kiss
and
Tell

How Far Is Too Far?

How far is too far? This is a question girls (and guys) have been asking themselves for decades, and although the times have changed, the answers are always the same. The only difference is people's openness in discussing sex due to the fact that we're bombarded by images of sexual indiscretion.

Many different viewpoints on the subject of sex are argued and argued well—thus the reason for mass confusion. Not only that, but we hear about various sexual encounters that leave us wondering, "What is sex and what is not sex?"

Girlfriend, sex is serious business. And although our culture has turned sex into a casual event, the consequences of nonchalant sex are severe.

In this chapter we're going to tackle the hype, hearsay, and horrors of sex with honest answers which will help you decide how far is too far. So if you're ready, let's take this subject a little bit farther.

Matter of Fact

The length of a relationship often determines how intimate you are. For example, a first date may end with a kiss while a month-long relationship starts with one. Here's something to think about: once you break up, will you be happy you kissed him at all? Yes, even a kiss can be a step too far.

What's in a kiss? A kiss is an act of affection shared with those we have special feelings for. So the question is, "How does that relate to that special someone in your life known as your boyfriend?" Is kissing him okay or isn't it? Some people find kissing harmless while others prefer to save it. What do

● ●

If you go too far too soon, you'll have regrets, but you'll never regret waiting for the right time.

Kiss and Tell

I mean by that? I'll let my friend Nicole, a nineteen-year-old sophomore in college, explain.

I met this really great guy a little over two years ago that I fell head-over-heels for. He is the kind of guy every girl dreams about: tall, dark, handsome, and every bit a gentleman. We hadn't been dating long when I seriously wondered if this was Mr. Right, the man of my dreams, the guy I would someday marry, which led me to start daydreaming about my wedding . . . *"You may kiss the bride."* That was it, the start of a lifelong relationship as man and wife; it all starts with the kiss. I determined right then and there that I would save the kiss until I heard those words. I shared my thoughts with Eric, and although he found it frustrating, he said his feelings for me were worth the wait. We remained devoted to one another, and then a year later we went off to separate colleges. We kept in touch every day via email and the phone, and we spent almost every waking minute of breaks together when I was home. During summer vacation we had a turning point in our relationship; we decided to break up but remain friends. And guess what? We are. We've remained awesome friends, and I believe that's because we never kissed. You see, physical intimacy would have left me with feelings of guilt, which in turn would have made it difficult to be friends with someone who was a constant reminder of past regrets. Now, I'm not saying that waiting to be kissed as a bride is the right thing for everyone, but from personal experience it's been the right thing for me. I'm glad, and so is Eric, that we didn't take our relationship too far.

Nicole's "no kissing" stand may seem a little rigid to you; however, I admire her for sticking to her standards. The bottom line is kissing is an act of physical intimacy, which often leads to more involved physical intimacy, which is something that shouldn't be shared with your boyfriend but saved for your groom.

Get a Clue

A kiss on the lips awakens our bodies to strange new sensual feelings that we've never felt before. It's like a nervous but exciting stimulation that makes you want to kiss again, and again, and again. The question is, where does all that kissing take you? For you, the girl, kissing and being held in the arms of that special someone is often enough, but for the guy it's usually a different story. Your emotional needs can be met just by feeling cared for by that special someone; however, remember what I said in chapter 2—it's not the same for the male species. Guys define care as a physical act, while girls define care by having their emotional needs met. So while you're happy with a kiss and a hug, the guy is already contemplating his next move.

So does this mean that kissing a guy is going too far? Well, let me put it this way: I learned this lesson the hard way.

Simplify

Before you get to the point where your life has been turned upside down because you went farther than you had planned, let me see if I can help by clarifying some of the hype, hearsay, and horrors of sexual activity with some simple honesty.

Hype

We are bombarded by sexual hype. It's everywhere we look—television, magazines, music videos, the Internet, movies, etc. Commercials use sexual advances to sell products; sitcoms make light of sex; and music videos indulge us with provocative dance moves. Everything seems to point to sex, indicating that everyone is doing it, or at least trying to. And then, of course, there are the rich and famous—music celebrities, movie stars, pro athletes, models, and political leaders—whose sexual activity outside of marriage is highly publicized, making it appear as a celebrated way of life. Oh, sure, we see the breakups and who's cheating on who on *Entertainment Tonight*, but we rarely get a look at the depression, fury, and emotional distress that take place away from the public eye. The fact is, these media images dull our senses and skew our thoughts regarding sexual activity. We're left with the impression that sex outside of marriage is acceptable and no consequences must be paid, unless of course you get caught.

The truth is, I've been to Hollywood and seen the pain, suffering, and heartache that goes on behind the scenes and when the cameras are off. You can't give away what was intended for husband and wife without becoming an emotional wreck. No one can avoid the consequences of sexual indiscretion, no matter who you are or who you aren't.

Hearsay

Sex is a hot topic, so sure, everyone is talking about it. The thing is, you have to wonder how much of what you hear is true and how much is just wishful thinking. For example, when a guy tells you everyone is doing it, he has ulterior motives. He's hoping that you won't want to be the only one who is not doing it. Or what about "locker room" talk? Guys and girls swap stories about who they've been with and how far they've gone. However, the majority of what you hear is a lie. Speaking of lies, let's talk about chat rooms for a moment. Online dating is all the rage. You can now live in California and "date" online a guy who lives in New York. This type of dating involves sitting at the computer for hours getting to know one another by instant messaging back and forth. Yet this is just one more place people lie and

Tammy's Tip

Guys don't like to be teased with a kiss.

lie big. Did you know that according to an informal survey I conducted, more than 78 percent of people lie about who they are online? So before you get caught up in cyber-dating, I'd suggest you take that into consideration.

Honestly, we put too much stock into hearsay. An old saying goes like this: "Believe nothing you hear and only half of what you see, and question everything." Apply that philosophy to hearsay about sex, and you'll feel a lot less pressure to live up to what others say is going on.

Horrors

Get your facts straight. Know the consequences of fooling around. Contrary to popular belief, STDs were not invented to scare you. They are for real, and yes, you are susceptible if you're sexually active. We always think these things only happen to other people—they could never happen to you, 'cuz you're invincible, right? Sorry to say it, but that's not true. It *can* happen to you, and with STDs at epidemic levels, if you're sexually active you have a better chance of contracting an STD than you do of contracting the flu. Remember, you're not only at risk because of the person you're sexually involved with but your risk multiplies when you factor in everyone else your partner has been with. The more people he's experimented with, the greater the chance he's acquired something he'll pass on to you. I could tell you horror story after horror story of girls who have gotten HIV, herpes, unwanted pregnancies, and other consequences, but I won't because for some reason we're basically unaffected by other people's stories. Only when it happens to you or someone very close to you does reality set in.

I hope you'll give some thought to what I am saying. I don't have anything to lose, but you do. I care what happens to you, and if I can spare you from becoming a statistic, then this book has been worth the effort. And if you're reading

this after learning the hard way, I hope you'll discover heal-
ing in the pages to follow.

FYI

These days a lot of confusion is out there about what sex
is and what sex isn't. For a clear definition, let's check out
the dictionary:

> **sex:** 1) sexual intercourse; 2) sexual activity or behavior
> leading to it

According to *Webster's*, sex is not the mere act of sexual
intercourse but also includes the activity surrounding it. That
means that sexual experiences of all types indicate a sexual
relationship. Sex is all about physical intimacy, and intimacy
is all about having a close personal relationship with another
person. That means that sexual relationships include oral sex,
bisexuality, three-ways, cybersex, and same-sex relationships. Even sexual encounters alone with a racy magazine or
Internet porn qualify as a sexual experience, although close
personal intimacy is absent.

Bottom line: sex is more than just the act of intercourse.
Having sex consists of all styles of sexual activity, and any
type of it is wrong and destructive outside of marriage. Sex
is reserved for husband and wife . . . PERIOD.

What's It 2U?

Understanding what sex is all about will help you know
how far is too far and es-
tablish limits now, before
your boundaries become
limitless.

Tammy's Tip

God is bigger than all our
mistakes and offers forgiveness
to anyone who asks.

Think your limits through now so you're not wishing you had later. Like I said before, I've met many girls with all kinds of horror stories regarding sex, but all of them have one common denominator between them—and that is that they all wish they had saved sex for marriage. Unfortunately, it's too late for them to learn from their mistakes. But it's not too late for you. You can learn this lesson the hard way and reap the consequences, or you can take the easy way out and receive the benefits. The choice is yours.

C4 Yourself

Sex is serious business. We may not give it much thought before it happens, but after the fact it plagues our minds with guilt, confusion, and worry. Many girls end up going too far because they don't realistically think about sex until it is too late. My advice is that you contemplate now what you want out of your future. Maybe you're like Nicole and want to save your kiss for your wedding day, or maybe you're planning on going to college and living in a dorm but know that can't happen if you become a teenage mom. The experts say that the more you're informed about "safe sex," the better off you are; however, although teenagers giving birth has declined, abortions and STDs have been on the rise, which to me would indicate that being informed about safe sex methods isn't working. Truthfully, the only safe sex is within the boundaries of marriage. You've got to have a (marriage) license to do it. So how far is too far? Too far is anything that opens the door to sexual activity before your wedding day.

Going the Distance

Going the distance refers to seeing something through. It means you're in it for the long haul, ready to endure the nasty

A self-disciplined life spares you from being disciplined with the consequences of your sin.

in order to be rewarded with the nice. Going the distance is all about setting goals in order to achieve the desired outcome; it's a state of mind that determines how your life is prioritized. For instance, passing history class involves studying for the tests, competing in gymnastics takes hours of practice, performing at a piano recital requires rehearsal, going to college means setting goals, and knowing how to avoid temptation calls for a certain amount of thinking ahead. It all comes down to cause and effect—putting forth the effort in order to achieve a desired objective. And to do that you first have to think about what you are going to do.

Life is all about opportunity—not waiting for it to happen but *making* it happen by planning for the future. Sometimes we like to think the way our lives play out is beyond our control, but we know that isn't necessarily true. Sure, some things we can't help, but that doesn't mean we can't change our thinking and take on positive attitudes that will change our perspective and help us develop an optimistic outlook.

Opportunity is achieved by applying discipline, which helps you organize yourself so that you can decide what to devote yourself to and what to divert yourself from, remembering in the process that your number one responsibility is to God.

Contrary to popular belief, life is *not* one big free-for-all, yet we are often driven by the moment with no thought of how our actions could affect the future. In fact, so much of what could have been is lost in the moment that was. And why? The problem starts when we fantasize about what life might become instead of realistically planning what it should be.

You can't have "safe sex" until you go as far as saying an official "I do."

Tammy's Tip

Casual sex is more than a short-term physical encounter; it's long-term emotional entrapment.

Matter of Fact

Now, don't take what I'm saying the wrong way. I don't think there is anything wrong with daydreaming, unless it causes you to think irrationally. For example, what about people who don't plan for their futures because they dream of winning the lottery someday? I know that sounds crazy, but unfortunately, a lot of people out there are depending on that very dream. Or what about the girl who romanticizes "happily ever after" with that special guy, convincing herself that she's going to marry him someday so having sex with him now is no big deal. The fact is, too much fantasizing can be a dangerous thing if it gets out of control.

Get a Life

How does fantasy affect your thinking? Does it help you establish goals and make plans, or does it warp your train

Time Out
with Tammy

All of us will do things we regret, and all of us will suffer consequences for making bad choices, some having a short-term effect, others having a lifelong impact. I've talked to girls all across the country who have changed the course of their lives just because they didn't take time to think first. I'd like to share one of those stories with you now.

Amber's Story

I was only fourteen years old and was secretly dating a twenty-year-old college sophomore. I ended up pregnant and decided to have an abortion. On the day of the scheduled abortion, I went alone, scared to death and not having any idea what I was doing. I don't remember much of the procedure; it's like I blanked it all out until the very end, when I just lay on the table crying, trying to muster up the energy to get myself home into bed. Later that evening my mom came in from work to find me burning up with fever and hemorrhaging. She immediately called my dad to meet us at the hospital. Once the examination was over and the diagnosis was made, my abortion was no longer a secret; it was a mistake gone wrong. My parents of thought? Remember, the way you live for God is directly related to the way you think, and the way you think is driven by your self-control or lack of it.

> Knowing God leads to self-control. Self-control leads to patient endurance, and patient endurance leads to godliness.
>
> 2 Peter 1:6 NLT

Everything you think, say, and do should be driven by your relationship with God, which will help strengthen your willpower so you can carry out his will. This growth process takes endurance in order to make you more Christlike. Living a godly life is a matter of discipline, and it all begins with a change of mind.

> Don't copy the behavior and customs of this world, but let God transform you into a new person by changing the way you think. Then you will know what God wants you to do,

were furious; in fact, they were so mad they made a claim against the abortion clinic and filed statutory rape charges against my boyfriend. He ended up serving jail time and lost his college scholarship, and I ended up losing my parents' trust, not to mention that I could have died from the abortion. It's been several years since this happened, and not one day has gone by that I have not remembered the death of my baby and regretted all my decisions surrounding the incident: dating someone I knew my parents wouldn't approve of, having sex before marriage, and aborting my baby. Mine was a series of bad choices that had a devastating impact on the guy, my parents, and me. This whole thing has tormented me for years. My unborn child haunts my mind, and as a result I battle depression and forgiveness. It's like I know God forgives me because I've prayed and asked him to, but I just can't forgive myself. I wish that I could go back to when I was fourteen and rethink what I was doing, because if I could, I wouldn't have this story to share or these memories to bear.

Girls, guard your minds. Think about how your choices will affect your future. Wise decisions today make for more contented tomorrows.

and you will know how good and pleasing and perfect his will
really is.

Romans 12:2 NLT

Self-control or self-discipline begins with proactive thinking. You must take initiative in your thought life in order
to live a disciplined, responsible life. Too many people ruin
what could have been with poor decision making. Living for
the moment instead of thinking things through has changed
the course of many lives.

Decisions affect all areas of our lives for either the good or
the bad. But probably the worst case scenario comes from not
thinking at all. We don't plan for our futures because we're
too preoccupied with the here and now, which often includes
our latest crush. Yes, girls, it's true—guys confuse our thought
processes. They make us do things we wouldn't and neglect
things we shouldn't. We get wrapped up in feelings instead
of looking at the facts. And the fact is, this is your life and
how you play it will determine your outcome. Every single
day you get up and face a new day of challenges and choices
that will affect your future and your finish. Your life is your
choice. You are at the age where your parents, try as they
might, have very little influence over what you choose to do
and what you choose to neglect. Your future is basically in
your hands. Sure, Christ will intervene on your behalf, like he
did, for example, in Amber's life; he spared her life physically,
but the emotional scars are still there. You can't play the game
of life haphazardly without hurting yourself or someone else.
Life is a race—run it faithfully and you can't lose.

The Simple Truth

Remember that in a race everyone runs, but only one person
gets the prize. You also must run in such a way that you will

win. All athletes practice strict self-control. They do it to win a
prize that will fade away, but we do it for an eternal prize. So run
straight to the goal with purpose in every step.

1 Corinthians 9:24–26 NLT

I am a speed walker, and although I don't compete, I still
practice and try to maintain a certain level of endurance.
My goal is to pace myself at a steady rate as I strive to go
the distance. I have to continually develop my self-control
and exercise some forethought in order to succeed. Speed
walking, like all other sports, requires focus, conditioning,
and discipline.

Life is much the same way. In fact, being part of life's race
is the biggest competition you will ever be in. Unlike sports,
where you can train for a while and then take a break, the
rat race we call life goes on 24/7. That means you are racing
around the clock to survive all that life dishes out. And like
training for a marathon, you can persevere through life by
focusing on your goals, conditioning your mind, and disciplining your behavior.

Focus

Don't lose focus. Center in on what you want out of life
and then set mini-goals that will help you achieve the prize.
Planning requires focus. For example, you don't just become
a cheerleader without prior training; it takes a series of steps
to make yourself ready for tryouts. And you don't get the
lead in a play without first focusing in on your character and
rehearsing your lines. In the same way, you won't protect
your purity if you don't focus on how to save it. Life is a
process of goals to be conquered in order to move to the next
level. As a Christian your primary focus should be to become
more like Christ, no matter what your other objectives in

life may be. And I promise you this: if you stay God-focused, you will end up a winner.

I have not yet reached my goal, and I am not perfect. But Christ has taken hold of me. So I keep on running and struggling to take hold of the prize.

Philippians 3:12 CEV

Condition

Training begins by conditioning your mind. It's a matter of willing yourself to do something and then disciplining yourself to do it. To succeed you have to drop the *T* from *can't* and change your mind to think *I CAN do anything*—which includes overcoming your weaknesses with the help of Christ who gives you strength.

I can do all things through Christ who strengthens me.

Philippians 4:13 NKJV

Athletes know what their weaknesses are, so they condition themselves to work through the low points in order to succeed at what they are doing. For example, if a marathon runner knows he loses speed at the six-mile point, then he will rely on determination to make it through until his second wind kicks in. Our everyday life is the same—we all have weaknesses that slow us down, and only by conditioning our minds with the Word of God and prayer will we overcome and succeed.

Discipline

Discipline that is used to direct, change, learn or train a behavior requires will of mind in order to achieve the desired benefit. This is a tough one, because most people want results without any form of sacrifice. Take dieting for example. A bazillion diet plans all offer the same thing—amazing results without depriving yourself of what you want to eat. They each offer an easy solution, and while it sounds good in theory, ask the average dieter how easy it really is when the cravings kick in. Developing discipline is all about exercising self-control in order to receive the desired award.

Discipline begins with will of mind; you have to decide before you can do. Even those with natural ability in a given area have to discipline themselves to follow through. Let's say you've got a knack for art. If you don't discipline yourself to develop your talent, it will remain idle and you will never get any better. Or what about your temptation to sin? Do you put yourself into compromising situations that weaken your will? Willpower is not about tempting yourself in order to overcome but about having the smarts to avoid temptation altogether in order to achieve. It would be crazy for a dieter to hang out in a bakery in order to avoid sweets, just like it's nuts to think you can hang at keg parties and avoid alcohol when bombarded by peer pressure.

> Invest in truth and wisdom, discipline and good sense, and don't part with them.
>
> Proverbs 23:23 CEV

Focus requires conditioning, and conditioning requires discipline. You can't have one without the other and expect positive results. Focus on the outcome, condition your mind to think about the goal, and discipline your behavior to produce the desired results. These combined ingredients make up self-control and allow you to go the distance without giving up.

Tammy's Tip

Self-control is not a case of mind over matter but of disciplining your mind with what matters most.

FYI

> The Scriptures say to God's children . . . "The Lord corrects the people he loves and disciplines those he calls his own." Be patient when you are being corrected! This is how God treats his children. Don't all parents correct their children? . . . Our human fathers correct us for a short time, and they do it as they think best. But God corrects us for our own good, because he wants us to be holy, as he is. It is never fun to be corrected. In fact, at the time it is always painful. But if we learn to obey by being corrected, we will do right and live at peace.
>
> Hebrews 12:5–7, 10–11 CEV

God proves his love through discipline. As a loving Father, he corrects us to bring us into obedience according to his Word. He is grieved when we misbehave, and I'm sure it saddens him to discipline us with the consequences of our sin. I know that as a mom I've never enjoyed punishing my children for inappropriate behavior, but I also know that if I didn't, I wouldn't be helping them mature into responsible young adults.

Don't mess with God. You cannot and will not escape the consequences of your sin. Either you discipline yourself to do what's right, or God will discipline you if you choose to do wrong.

What's It 2U?

Opportunity is boosted through discipline. When you apply self-control you can achieve just about anything you put your mind to. The key is to not only discipline yourself to do what you need to do in order to reach your goal but also exercise moral self-control so that you don't miss out. Just like if you don't apply yourself in school, getting into the college of your choice will be difficult at best, if you tamper with sin, you may miss out on your goals altogether. I know girls who have changed the course of their lives with alcohol, drugs, theft, sex, and other temptations, and as a result they have never met their full potential.

Life is a series of circumstances that cause you to make choices—some big and some small, some serious and some not so serious, but all with end results. The fact is, it's up to you to manage your life by managing your mind. The way you think and what drives your thoughts will determine how you respond to life's toughest issues. Improve your thinking with the Word of God, and you will improve the quality of your life.

C4 Yourself

What makes you tick? Do you allow outside influences such as peer pressure, the media, or music to make up your mind and mood, or are you in control of what's going on in your head? Life is all about equipping your cranium with right thoughts, and to do that you have to read God's Word and apply it. A disciplined life begins with a disciplined mind. You are what you think. Going the distance is a state of mind. Think straight so you never have to hear or ask yourself, *"What were you thinking?!"*

Get a head start in your thinking to get ahead in life.

• •

Be TRUE to YOU—Discipline
yourself, and God won't need to.

Is
S-E-X
a Four-Letter Word?

What's Love Got to Do with It?

Sex is not love and love is not sex, and neither should be used as a bargaining tool in order to get what you want out of a relationship. For example, often girls will have sex to feel loved and guys will declare their love in order to have sex, but the problem is, both are done with selfish motives.

Love and sex are often used synonymously, yet they have very little in common without the missing link—*commitment*. Love without commitment does not equal sex, and sex without commitment does not equal love. The operative word here is *commitment*. Sex is about a commitment to love in the married sense of the word, "until death do us part," and physical intimacy in any other case does not equal commitment but consequences.

In case you have not figured it out by now, love and sex can be ultra confusing. They both involve feelings and trying to fulfill natural desires, but neither one complements the other without a vow to commitment. This is what this chapter is all about: helping you sort through the confusion and find truthful answers to perplexing questions about sex, love, and security.

Girl, love is a mystifying emotion. It makes you blind, deaf, and mute: blind to faults, deaf to negatives, and mute when it comes to voicing your own opinion in fear of rejection. The other thing about love is that it introduces feelings you have never felt before. It awakens a yearning for closeness—not necessarily of a sexual nature but often of a snuggling kind that signifies, "You're someone special that

Sex does not secure love; it complicates emotions.

I deeply care for." To girls snuggling offers security, but to guys snuggling mostly implies you are one step closer to having sex. I've said it before and I'll say it again: girls and guys think and respond differently. Girls are looking to be loved, and guys are looking to be physically satisfied.

Matter of Fact

An old saying goes like this: "Why buy the cow when you can get the milk for free?" In other words, why should a guy invest in what he can have for nothing? Something cheap is not appreciated, but the more something costs you, the more you value it.

Get a Clue

Establish a value system, beginning with yourself, because if you don't, no one else will. How you esteem yourself is how others will esteem you. This relates to all areas of life, especially sex.

I recently took a survey to find out what girls think about sex. One of the questions I asked was, "What do you expect to receive from sex?" Out of those who answered, 93 percent responded with "commitment." I also asked if they had been or were currently involved with someone sexually, and 34 percent responded yes, they were or had been sexually active. The final question on the questionnaire was, "If you've had sex, did it fulfill what you stated you expected or wanted in the question above?" Only 2 percent said, "Yes, it was what I expected or wanted," and, interestingly enough, out of that 2 percent only 1 person had said commitment was what they wanted. Bottom line, sex doesn't

Tammy's Tip

Your virginity is priceless; it's a sacred gift and should be protected at all costs.

lead to commitment. Girls have sex to hold onto their guy, and statistics show, *IT DOESN'T WORK!*

Having sex to keep a guy is craziness, but stats show that this is the primary reason girls give in to a guy's coercing. In fact, the majority of girls I polled said that they really didn't want to have sex at all but were scared into it by the threat of being dumped. When you have sex to try to save a relationship, you'll lose your self-respect and receive nothing but guilt.

Simplify

So many myths are out there regarding sex that it's hard to sort through all the propaganda in order to figure out what the truth truly is. I've heard many real-life scenarios, examples, and warnings. I've been preached at, lectured to, and instructed on sex, but nothing has been as relevant as what I'm about to share. The following acrostic on S-E-X is borrowed from my dear friend Rose Sweet.

S—Surrender Yourself to God

Dear friends, God is good. So I beg you to offer your bodies to him as a living sacrifice, pure and pleasing. That's the most sensible way to serve God.

Romans 12:1 CEV

The very first step to understanding sex comes in the form of surrendering to God. We think about surrender as a whole, like surrendering to a call or a mission, yet we rarely consider yielding individual areas of our life to God. But we need to. Turn the matter of sex over to God. Ask him to guide you, direct you, and help you not only avoid but also resist temptation in this area of your life. Remember, God wants the best for you, so ask him to help you wait to get it.

E—Educate Yourself with the Truth

Let God change the way you think. Then you will know how to
do everything that is good and pleasing to him.
Romans 12:2 CEV

Get smarter where sex is concerned. Educate yourself with
the truth; starting with the nitty-gritty facts found in Scripture. A lot of information on sex education is out there, and
it's up to you to figure out right from wrong by comparing
the information you gather from the world with what God
has to say about sex in his Word.

Special Note: There is one and ONLY one surefire method
of safe sex, and that is *no sex at all*. Abstinence is the key.

X—Cross Out (X Out) What the World's Telling You about Sex

Don't be like the people of this world.
Romans 12:2 CEV

You need to X out the world's point of view concerning
sex. The movies lie, the television distorts, magazines fib,
and public education misguides about sex. You can't trust
the world on this topic because Satan influences the world's
opinion. Satan is the father of lies and untruths (read John
8:44), and his job is to get you to go against God's ways so that
he can destroy you. God created sex for husband and wife,
so of course, Satan will encourage you to engage in sexual
activity outside the parameters of marriage. Satan wants to
turn God's best for you into painful consequences, because
his goal is to make your life miserable. Claim the power of the
cross, remembering that
Jesus "crossed out" Satan
there.

Tammy's Tip
Never fall into bed with a guy
hoping to get him to fall for you.

Is S-E-X a Four-Letter Word?

FYI

Sex should never be used selfishly. Don't take advantage of a guy by using sex to manipulate him into giving you what you want. Guys are known for thinking with their hormones and not their heads, and unfortunately many girls use this to their benefit. A girl will make herself available, hoping to catch the guy to use him for whatever goal she is working toward. For example, I've known girls who have intentionally become pregnant so they could trap the guy into marriage. And let me tell you, this fantasy *NEVER* works out as planned. Grudges are formed from the get-go, betrayal is inevitable, and trust, the basis for any relationship, is non-existent. Even if the guy marries you, the chances are next to none that it will last.

Remember, true love is not selfish, does not use others, and does not get even, but instead it protects, honors, and cherishes the object of its affection (see 1 Corinthians 13, known as the love chapter of the Bible).

True love waits to get married.

What's It 2U?

Sex can cost you more than you are willing to spend when you sell yourself short. Even girls who are engaged and committed to getting married regret having premarital sex with their fiancé because it leaves them riddled with guilt. Worse than that, those feelings of guilt often carry over into marriage, hindering what should have been a beautiful, strong, and wonderful physical bond between husband and wife.

The moral of the story? Be patient and wait your turn, and remember, God isn't trying to keep you from something good—he wants to give you something great!

C4 Yourself

Girl, be prepared to hear this from a guy: "If you love me, you'll show me." And be prepared to answer him with, "It's because I do care for you that I won't."

Don't confuse true love with self-centered love. True love is about continuous commitment, and selfish love is about self-gratification. True love is putting the other person first, and selfish love is about "me first." True love waits, but self-centered love wants instant gratification.

What's Vows Got to Do with It?

A vow is a solemn promise, a pledge to give, save, or abstain from something. A promise kept is of highest value to the recipient, but a broken promise betrays trust and hurts those involved. Vows are serious business and shouldn't be taken or given lightly, and by no means should they be used as a bargaining tool in order to get what you want. In fact, promising nothing at all is better than making a promise and breaking it.

Vows are made for many reasons but most commonly in the name of love. Some of these vows are genuine and some are not. The question is, how can you tell the difference? The answer is found in commitment. Commitment is the sincerest form of a vow. It loves unconditionally, through the good times and bad, never ending but growing stronger over time. Commitment is not merely something you say but something you do. The greatest example of this is God's love for us. He's vowed to love us yesterday, today, and forever, and he does. His love never quits.

Promises these days are confusing; they offer no guarantees. You don't know who to trust or how

Tammy's Tip

If you think you can trick someone into loving you, the only one you're fooling is yourself.

to trust, so you often get mistreated as you try to discern between reality and romanticism—the difference between "real" truth and what we "romanticize" the truth to be.

We girls are famous for falling for the words we want to hear, whether or not they are true. We love the thought of romance, and when we are in the throes of it we have a hard time discerning truth. We become confused between right and wrong, true and false, and good and bad. In a way, we become our own worst enemy when it comes to using good judgment. When the opposite sex whispers "sweet nothings" in our ears, we turn them into "sweet somethings"—they say one thing, and we hear another.

Matter of Fact

Guys and girls both are guilty of manipulating words and their meanings in order to get what they want. They'll pledge most anything in the moment, but after all is said and done forget what they vowed, which hurts everyone involved. Bottom line: empty words make empty promises, and empty promises lead to lack of trust.

Time Out
with Tammy

Have you ever lied to yourself or let yourself be lied to in order to get what you wanted? Or have you ever trusted in your own judgment, whether right or wrong, to get your own way? I sure have, and it was all because I trusted what I *wanted* to be the right thing for selfish reasons instead of what I *knew* to be the right thing according to the Bible. I justified it by trusting my feelings rather than facts so that I could manipulate my circumstances to get what I wanted. Only getting what I wanted wasn't what I got. Instead I got what I deserved.

Have you ever been so desperate for a guy that you would say or do just about anything to keep him? I have. I willingly traded my virtue for the sake of keeping the guy, even though deep inside I knew his sincerity was questionable. But like so many girls, I wanted what he was saying to be true, and I wanted him to be true to

Get a Life

Trust is what lasting relationships are built upon; with it you feel secure, and without it you're made to feel vulnerable. Trust is built when you mean what you say and do what you've said. The fact is, our commitment to our words either strengthens our integrity or destroys our character.

In order to save your purity—your most precious wedding gift for your groom-to-be—*VOW NOW* to make it happen. If you've already been sexually active, you can turn things around by asking God's forgiveness and vowing to remain abstinent from this day forward. Not sure it's worth the effort? Well, allow me to let you in on a poll I recently took among some high school and college age guys.

Guys, if you could receive one and only one wedding gift from your bride, what would you choose as most important to you?

a) the sports car of my dreams
b) season tickets to my favorite sports team
c) big bucks
d) the gift of my bride's virginity

me even if it meant that I wasn't being true to myself or my relationship with God. I operated off of feelings instead of facts and lied to myself by pretending everything was okay as long as he said he loved me.

I permitted myself to become a victim of my own circumstances by romanticizing the truth into what I wanted it to be. I was desperate to believe this guy's pledge of undying love so that I could feel "secure" in the relationship, even though it was obviously driven by selfish motives. Yes, I learned the hard way that guys are willing to promise just about anything to get their way with you. The fact is, I allowed myself to be used for the sake of a half-hearted commitment, which was what I thought I wanted, but the end result was extreme guilt. I speak from experience when I say *NOTHING* is worth your purity except an exchange of vows.

The answer from 100 percent of the guys was *d) the gift of my bride's virginity.* With that in mind, you can commit (or recommit) to saving it until what will be one of the most memorable occasions of your life—your wedding day. Are you ready to make the vow now?

VOW NOW

I, _____, VOW NOW here in the sight of God to commit (or recommit) myself from this day forward to guard my purity, so that I might save this exceptional gift until my wedding day to be shared with the man God has chosen especially for me, the man of my dreams, my groom.

Signed: _____ Date: _____

I pray that God will help you live up to your commitment to purity.

The Simple Truth

Vows are confusing. Politicians make and break promises daily, well-known companies back their products with false guarantees, and husbands and wives terminate their wedding vows with a certificate of divorce. With all of these broken pledges, how on earth are we supposed to understand the value of a vow, and what does a vow have to do with commitment and sex?

V—Value Your Commitment

Don't allow love to turn into lust, setting off a downhill slide into sexual promiscuity, filthy practices, or bullying greed.

Ephesians 5:3 Message

The very first step to honoring your vow is valuing your commitment to it. A vow is a solemn promise that declares to either abstain from something or to give something, and in the case of sex you are vowing to do both—to abstain from it until you can give it away on your wedding day. *Vow now to value your commitment to purity between God, yourself, and your groom-to-be.*

O—Own Your Convictions

God wants you to live a pure life. Keep yourselves from sexual promiscuity. Learn to appreciate and give dignity to your body, not abusing it, as is so common among those who know nothing of God.

1 Thessalonians 4:3–5 Message

It's up to you to take ownership of your convictions, and with God's help you can do it. You are responsible for how you handle yourself and your moral principles. Your purity is your business, and unless someone forceably takes it from you, you own it and only you can give it away. Decide today what you believe and why you believe it, and then stand on those ideas. *Vow now to own your convictions regarding intimacy between God, yourself, and your future mate.*

W—Watch Out for Compromises

Watch out for the Esau syndrome: trading away God's lifelong gift in order to satisfy a short-term appetite.

Hebrews 12:16 Message

Beware of compromising situations! Carefully plan how to avoid them before they happen, and in case one takes you by surprise, be ready to respond with an emergency prayer for help out of it.

Vow now to watch out for compromising circumstances that could hinder your relationship with God and your future husband.

● ●

FYI

Be TRUE to YOU—A pledge to purity promises passionate living.

The Bible says it's better not to make a vow than to promise something and not keep it. So does that mean you should never make any promises? No, but it does mean that you shouldn't enter into a vow halfheartedly. You should only make a promise if your intentions are on the up-and-up. For example, say you promise your mom you'll clean your room if she'll let you go to the mall with your friends, so she says yes, and off you go. Two days later your mom says, "I thought you were going to clean your room," and you say, "Oh yeah, I forgot." Now the question is, did you forget, or did you make an empty promise so you could get your own way? It all comes down to your intent.

What are your intentions? Do you make promises with the intent to keep your word, or do you make promises to get your way? You should only make a vow if you intend to follow through with whatever it is you've committed to, and if you do otherwise, you are in the wrong. The Bible tells us point blank not to make a promise that we don't intend to keep, but what happens if you commit to a promise with the best of intentions and break it anyway? That's where God's forgiveness and grace come in. As long as you truly repent, God will forgive and forget. True repentance means that you not only ask God's forgiveness but also do a U-turn and run the opposite direction from your sin.

Maybe you've already made a promise to purity and broke that commitment. Well, guess what? God is the God of second, third, and even fourth chances. If you ask him to restore your virginity, I truly believe he will renew your purity of mind.

Here's a warning, however: don't play in the revolving door of repentance. What do I mean by that? I mean don't do the same thing over and over again with the mind-set of, "I'll just ask God to forgive me again and again." Don't keep going in circles. When you enter into forgiveness, exit away from your sin. Remember, sincere repentance brings true forgiveness.

What's It 2U?

A broken vow may mean nothing to you unless you are on the receiving end of it, but then it means everything. Being able to take someone at their word is critical to forming lasting relationships. Never commit to someone you can't trust. A commitment to one's word is the basis of trust, and without it you have no foundation for a meaningful relationship.

Words to live by: honor your word and you'll honor your name; or break your promises and you'll ruin your reputation.

C4 Yourself

Love, vows, and commitment are confusing, especially since God created us for relationships—a relationship with him first and then relationships with others. When you get your vertical relationship (between you and God) right, your horizontal relationships (between you and other people) will move in the right direction also. Your God-connection should be your number one priority, your number one commitment, and when it is, it will influence all other relationships in your life. Your love for God should be your motivation for obedience to him, and your respect for God should be your incentive to uphold your vow to sexual purity.

Tammy's Tip

Passion without promise is like chocolate without sugar—it leaves you bitter.

Sexual Revelation

What Your Mother Didn't Tell You

As I travel around the country I hear from many moms on the topic of sex. Obviously, they don't need to know about it, because after all, they've managed to have you. But what they do want to know is how to approach you about the subject.

Sex can be an uncomfortable topic of discussion for both mother and daughter. There's just something about the issue of sex that makes you feel awkward where your parents are concerned. You don't like to discuss it with them and surprise! They don't like to discuss it with you either. You have your reasons and they have theirs. Yet you each may have some questions and concerns you'd like to have answered and discussed, but no one has the nerve to initiate a conversation or invade one another's silence on the subject.

Well, I'm about to break the silence. I've spent the last several months gathering information on sex from moms just like yours across the nation. They have been open and honest about sharing what they want you to know about sex and exactly why they want you to know it. The following pages are filled with true life stories about sex; however, the places and names have been omitted in order to keep the mothers and their families from experiencing unnecessary embarrassment.

Girl, hear me now: your mom was once a girl just like you. Finding that hard to comprehend? Well, it's true, and like you, she had unanswered questions about sex that her mother didn't address either. In fact, in her day sex was less talked about than it is now. Like you,

● ● ● ● ● ● ● ● ● ● ● ● ● ● ● ● ●

Experience is often the mother of advice.

she probably got her information second- and third-hand from her friends or possibly learned it firsthand for herself. Either way, that was then and this is now, and today she can speak from experience. She knows the subject well and wants to share with you what she has learned about sex.

Matter of Fact

Speaking from a mom's perspective, I can tell you point blank that the main reason we don't openly discuss sex with you is because it puts us in a compromising situation. We want to share with you what we've learned but not necessarily how we've learned it. Some of our experiences make us feel vulnerable, and we're afraid you will think less of us or take on the attitude, "You learned about it your way, so why shouldn't I?"

Maybe you're sitting here thinking, "Tammy, it's not that way with my mom and me. We tell each other everything." And if that's the case, great, but it's not the norm. Most moms I've spoken with have avoided talking about sex with their daughters, which is why I've included this chapter as a safe place for moms to open up and be brutally honest on the topic of sex.

Get a Life

The following stories are written to you from moms who have personally found out the truth about sex and purity and how they affect you both now and in the future. Read the following letters and learn from them.

Tammy's Tip

Not sure how to bring up the hot topic of sex with your parents? Use an icebreaker question such as, "Mom, how did you first learn about the birds and the bees?"

Dear Daughter,

When I was your age, I didn't have a clue about sex. The mere mention of the word was taboo in our family. From what I gathered from my mother, it was a dirty little subject that shouldn't be brought up or discussed openly. The only thing I ever heard was, "Don't have it until you're married," and that was it. Unfortunately, I never understood why that advice was given until it was too late.

You see, I had sex before I was married, not knowing or understanding that there would be consequences for my behavior. At first it seemed fine. I couldn't figure out what the big deal was; after all, I didn't even like it. The truth is, I only put out to keep my boyfriend from finding someone else who would. Several months into the relationship I discovered I was pregnant. I went to my boyfriend and told him, and he was furious, like it was my fault and he had nothing to do with it. He even went as far as saying, "It can't be mine," knowing all along that was a lie. We talked over the next several days about how we would tell our parents or if we should run away together and not tell them at all. It ended up that we did neither because I had a miscarriage. It was horrible.

Although it was a baby I didn't want, the loss was more than I could bear. And my boyfriend's response of happy relief really did me in. He was downright thrilled that our baby had died prematurely. Those were the darkest days of my life. The hurt and pain, both mentally and emotionally, were more than I could stand, and as a result I slipped into a deep depression and no one but my (now) ex-boyfriend and me knew why. Sex before marriage tore me up inside. I wished I had died with my baby and even contemplated suicide. This is the reason I'm so adamant about abstinence. I pray you'll learn from my mistakes and avoid the hurt of your own.

With Love,
Miscarriage Mom

Sexual Revelation

To My Girls,

Today it seems like there is a lot of information floating around about abstinence and virginity but not nearly enough on purity. Purity is more than being a virgin; it's all about refraining from any type of sexual activity before marriage. It includes everything from touching and caressing to Internet porn and oral sex. Purity is a physical condition as well as a state of mind. Protect your thinking and pray for wisdom as you're dealing with curiosity.

When I was thirteen I looked at and read the first of many porn magazines. I became addicted to them, and if I wasn't reading one, I was rehearsing in my mind what I'd read. I'd never actually had sex in a physical manner, but mentally I had it hundreds of times. It warped my viewpoint on sex and as a result adversely affected my thinking long into the future. Once you get that stuff in your mind, it's hard to get it out. Even today, years later, it's there, imbedded deep in my mind, wanting to creep to the forefront and take over my thought life. Girls, my prayer for you is that you'll guard your thinking and protect your purity.

Thinking of You,
Reminded Mom

Honey,

I don't know where to start, so I guess I'll start at the beginning. When I first met your dad, I knew he was the one for me; it was definitely love at first sight. We had only dated three months when we started talking marriage, and within no time we were "pre-engaged." As our commitment to each other intensified, so did our physical relationship, and although I had convictions about saving sex for marriage, I eventually gave in to your father's coercing. Extreme guilt plagued me each and every time we had sex before we were married. The problem is, the guilt never stopped. Once we were married, the feeling that I was doing something wrong never went away. In fact, it intensified to the point where I was turned off sexually, which in turn was destroying our marriage. We've since received professional counseling that I hope will undo what the last sixteen years of guilt has done.

What I'm trying to say is that a few seconds of premarital pleasure is not worth the ongoing consequences. Please be encouraged to wait until you're married before you get intimately involved.

With Love and Concern,
Mother of Guilt

Simplify

Quite often the reason mothers are so overprotective is because they want to save you from making the same mistakes they made. I hear what you're saying—*"I'm not my mother, and just because she made bad choices doesn't mean I will."* True, but that doesn't mean you won't either, and perhaps someday you'll be in your mother's shoes, teaching your kids what you learned from life's experiences. Heeding your mother's advice doesn't mean you won't make mistakes, but I hope you will listen and learn from her as much as you possibly can.

FYI

Moms aren't the only ones who have something to say about sex. Dads do too. It seems, however, that when it comes to boys, dating, and sex many fathers become flustered discussing these things with their little girls. They remember all too well what it was like being a teenage boy, and as a result they become overprotective, trying to save you from what they knew at your age.

Have you ever heard horror stories of a dad intimidating his daughter's date when the guy arrived to pick her up? Maybe it's even happened to you. But have you ever wondered *why* a dad would express such irrational behavior? It's because he knows how guys think and act where girls, dating, and sex are concerned. Your dad was once a teenage boy himself, one with raging hormones that were hard to control—thus the reason he freaks when you want to date. Understand this: it's not that your dad doesn't trust you; it's that he doesn't trust the guy who wants to date you. Your father has your best interests in mind. He just has a funny way of showing it. So the next time your boyfriend comes to the door and your dad gives him the third degree—asking everything from, "Have you ever had a speeding ticket?" to "Did you know I have a blackbelt in karate?"—grin and bear it, knowing you're daddy's little girl and he wants to protect you at all costs.

What's It 2U?

I don't want to make excuses for how your parents parent you, but I do want to offer up some insight as to why they are more passionate about some things than others: it's based on their knowledge and experience. For example, my husband was in a serious car accident that could have killed him had he not been wearing his seatbelt. Prior to the accident he had no convictions either way about buckling up, but after the accident he became fanatical about getting in the car and fastening his seatbelt before he started the ignition. Even though the seatbelt law wasn't in

Tammy's Tip

Talk to your parents. They understand way more than you give them credit for.

effect at the time of the accident, the government did strongly encourage the use of seatbelts for the purpose of saving lives. We didn't understand the importance of this suggestion until it affected us directly, and once it did, we became zealous over the value found in wearing a seatbelt.

Parents get passionate over some issues more than others because they've been directly or indirectly affected by them in some way. A set of circumstances in their lives led to their strong convictions on that matter. That's not to say that every single rule or guideline they give is based on something that happened to them, but you can pretty much be certain that the rules they are most adamant about were made as a result of something they learned from their past. I for one am very passionate about group dating because the few times

Time Out
with Tammy's Mom

As I mentioned in chapter 2, I was adopted when I was in third grade. But that's only part of the story. In this "Time Out" I've asked my mom to revisit her past and share with you what she learned the hard way so that you, like me, can learn from her mistakes and live a better life.

Dear Readers,

I was raised in a loving home where spousal abuse was unheard of, and I suppose the fact that I had never been exposed to it made me naive to its existence.

When I was dating I was too much in love to recognize any tendencies toward abuse my future husband (Tammy's birth father) might have had before we got married. I blindly married into my own personal war, which took place behind closed doors for more than seven years.

I had been married less than a month when my husband beat me up for the first time. I was devastated and threatened to leave him, but with tears running down his face, he apologized, begged me to stay, and vowed never to hit me again. Wanting to live "happily ever after," I forgave him and agreed to stay, but within two weeks the beatings resumed. The battering became more severe, and the aftermath was always the same—bruises for me and promises from him to never do it again. The physical abuse backed up by mental manipulation had convinced me that I

I did single date made me highly uncomfortable. My teenagers will tell you that I've tried to persuade them from the
get-go to avoid pairing off until they are ready for that kind
of responsibility. As a mom I don't want them to have to
experience what I learned the hard way.

You may feel like your parents are punishing you for their
mistakes, but in reality they are just trying to save you from
them. What about you? Is there anything you've learned
firsthand that you would like to warn others about? Think
about it. Your lesson learned could save someone else the
grief of learning it for herself. Your parents are not necessarily trying to make life harder for you. Actually the opposite
is true: they just want you to be smarter about growing up
than they were.

deserved each and every beating I received. I felt trapped, like there was no way
out, until finally he left and I reached out for help.

Girls, if I can impress one thing upon you, it's that should you find yourself in an
abusive relationship of any kind, GET OUT and GET HELP! No one deserves to be
treated this way! Abusers, like leopards, don't change their spots without outside
assistance. Any person who abuses another doesn't have a clue as to what real
love is all about; not only do they not love you but they also don't respect you.
These people cannot be trusted, and without trust you have no basis for a
relationship.

Remember, God fashioned Eve from Adam's rib to be a helpmate at his side. Had
God intended Eve to assume the position of a doormat, he would have created her
from Adam's foot. No one deserves to be abused!

Sincerely,
(Tammy's) Mom

Girlfriend, should you find yourself in an abusive situation of *any kind*, GET
HELP NOW! Don't wait another minute. Call the National Abuse Hotline at 1-800-
799-7233.

C4 Yourself

I know from past personal experience that it's hard to talk to your parents about sex. That's one reason I'm writing this book! I want you to understand what I never understood until I was married with children of my own. Parents are people too. They have made mistakes and hopefully learned from them, and now they want to help you avoid what they've already learned. They aren't party poopers trying to rid you of fun; they are on a mission from God.

Parental Mission: "Point your kids in the right direction—when they're old they won't be lost" (Prov. 22:6 Message).

What Your Father Wants You to Know

There's nothing sweeter than a father/daughter relationship—one built on trust, honesty, and understanding; one that protects, guides, directs, and nurtures; one that never fails. And there's only one that lives up to those standards: the one you can have with God the Father. Everyone longs for a relationship like this, and although anyone who seeks can have it, few are committed to finding it.

This Father/daughter bond cannot compare to anything else because God listens, leads, and loves like no other. He wants you to talk to him about boys, dating, and sex, because after all, he created them. No one knows more about these topics than God, and no one has better answers on these subjects than him. So what do you have to lose? Go ahead, ask away. God wants to hear all your questions.

Let's revisit the letters written by our moms and find out what God has to say about the situations. Of course, hindsight is always 20/20, but God's foresight is even better than our hindsight. You see, hindsight has consequences after the fact,

Parents establish rules
to give you freedom.

but foresight spares you the aftermath of regretting what could have been. Read on. You'll see just what I'm talking about.

Have you ever wished you could go back and do something over again? I have. Many times I've found myself wishing I could go back and do something I hadn't done, undo something I did, say something I didn't say, or take back something I said. And why? Because knowing what you should have done is easier than figuring out what you should do.

Human hindsight clearly shows you the past, but godly foresight clarifies the future.

Matter of Fact

Like I said earlier, sex was less talked about in your mom's day than it is in yours. In fact, back then she had a lot less info available on STDs, teen pregnancy, date rape, etc. But one thing has not changed, and that's the Bible. Sure, there are newer versions out and about, but God's Word pertaining to guys, dating, sex, and everything else is the same yesterday, today, and forever.

> People are like grass that dies away; their beauty fades as quickly as the beauty of wildflowers. The grass withers, and the flowers fall away. But the word of the Lord will last forever.
>
> 1 Peter 1:24–25 NLT

Times change, consequences vary, but God's standard for a rich and full life remains the same. That means that your mom and grandma were expected to live by the same biblical standards you are today. Nothing has changed as far as God is concerned. His biblical truths apply now just as they applied then.

Tammy's Tip

Feel blessed if you have parents who get a little screwy when you date. Not every girl is that fortunate.

Sexual Revelation

Get a Life

Go back to page 162 and read the first letter, the one from Miscarriage Mom. Let it sink in and then come back here.

You cannot fool God, so don't make a fool of yourself! You will harvest what you plant. If you follow your selfish desires, you will harvest destruction, but if you follow the Spirit, you will harvest eternal life.

Galatians 6:7–8 CEV

It's a law of nature: you reap what you sow. If you plant watermelon seeds, don't expect daisies! The same rule applies to other areas of life too. If you have premarital sex, expect consequences, because every action, good or bad, produces appropriate results.

God designed sex for husband and wife, and anything outside of that is in violation of God's divine design. Whenever you deviate from God's perfect plan and start making up your own rules, you can expect less than perfect results.

Miscarriage Mom is a prime example of what happens when we do things the world's way instead of following God's Word.

The good news is: God has forgiven this mom for her actions.

The bad news is: She has not forgotten the results of her sin.

Forgiving and forgetting are two different things. God forgives and forgets, but we remember and feel shame.

Next let's consider the letter from Reminded Mom. Go to page 163 and read it over again.

Sexual Revelation

> God has called us to be holy, not to live impure lives.
> Anyone who refuses to live by these rules is not disobeying
> human rules but is rejecting God, who gives his Holy Spirit
> to you.
>
> 1 Thessalonians 4:7–8 NLT

Looking at porn and fantasizing over what you see and read warps your senses and responses toward sex. Porn portrays a degrading and unrealistic ideal of sexual intimacy that can lead to destructive behavior. It not only creates a poor self-image in the individual it traps but also encourages sexual gratification, which lowers a person's self-worth. I have counseled those involved in this type of behavior, and each and every person I've talked to has been down on themselves, full of shame, depressed, and riddled with guilt, wanting to stop but feeling trapped by the mental visions that are filed away in their brains.

Unfortunately, Reminded Mom has learned about the penalty of porn the hard way; once it's in there, it's almost impossible to get it out. Mental images become engraved in our brains, and the only way to erase them is to give the mind a new assignment. The absolute best homework to clear up your thought process is to read and memorize the Bible! It's like taking a glass of muddy water and pouring clean water into it—the more clean water you pour into the glass, the more the muddy water will disperse until it's all cleared up.

The good news is: God has forgiven Reminded Mom for her sexual addiction.

The bad news is: The images she filled her head with then would like to re-emerge in her mind today.

God doesn't keep record of our sins, but they are recorded in our brains as a constant reminder of what not to do again.

Once again, before you go on, go back to page 163 to reread what Mother of Guilt has to say.

> I want you to promise, O women of Jerusalem, not to awaken love until the time is right.
>
> Song of Solomon 8:4 NLT

Sex before its time has damaging effects. You can't buck God's system without paying the price. And sometimes the cost is higher than what we expected. In this particular case, Mother of Guilt expected the consequences to fade away once she was married, but as you have read, they further developed and created division between her and her husband. You cannot modify God's plan for intimacy in marriage, but you can spoil it. The fact is, sex before its time can screw up your future.

The good news is: God has forgiven Mother of Guilt for her past.

The bad news is: Mother of Guilt has to work through her past mistakes in order to enjoy her future.

When you try to jump ahead of God's plan you end up behind with a problem.

One more letter—the one from my mom. Read it over in the "Time Out" section on page 166.

> However, each one of you also must love his wife as he loves himself, and the wife must respect her husband.
>
> Ephesians 5:33 NIV

Like my mom said, God created Eve from Adam's rib to be by his side, not from his feet to be his doormat. No guy has the right to abuse you on any level—not physically, emotionally, mentally, or verbally. All forms of abuse are wrong. Love (for God and for each other), trust, and respect are the basis for any relationship, and if you find yourself in one based on anything else, end it before it's too late.

The good news is: My mom came to know the Lord after the abuse.

The bad news is: The emotional damage led to low self-esteem, which led to excessive weight gain that has been a problem for my mom ever since.

The Simple Truth

The Word of God has answers to questions you didn't think to ask as well as those you've wondered about and still need answers to.

> Every part of Scripture is God-breathed and useful one way or another—showing us truth, exposing our rebellion, correcting our mistakes, training us to live God's way.
>
> 2 Timothy 3:16 Message

The Bible is a complete guide for life. It answers our most pressing questions. As I've traveled across the country and spoken to girls just like you, I've asked them, "What would you like me to talk about?" And repeatedly the two most common topics/questions have been: 1) *What kind of guy should I marry?* and 2) *What does the Bible*

Tammy's Tip

Be careful of finding porn in unexpected places. For example, some store catalogs use porn as a marketing tool to sell product.

say about premarital sex? Let's look at what the Bible says about these things.

What kind of guy should I marry?

A husband should love his wife as much as Christ loved the church and gave his life for it.

Ephesians 5:25 CEV

Now read the same verse in *The Message* paraphrase:

Husbands, go all out in your love for your wives, exactly as Christ did for the church—a love marked by giving, not getting.

Ephesians 5:25 Message

God loves you so much that he allowed his Son to die on your behalf. Jesus Christ gave his life to save you. That's the kind of husband you're looking for—one who loves you and will defend you at any price, even if it costs him his life.

What does the Bible say about premarital sex?

Since we want to become spiritually one with the Master, we must not pursue the kind of sex that avoids commitment and intimacy, leaving us more lonely than ever—the kind of sex that can never "become one." There is a sense in which sexual sins are different from all others. In sexual sin we violate the sacredness of our own bodies, these bodies that were made for God-given and God-modeled love, for "becoming one" with another.

1 Corinthians 6:17–18 Message

Premarital sex can never satisfy God's design for intimacy. Our commitment should be to God first and foremost so we can become one with him, allowing him to meet our need for a close relationship. Anything that detracts from God's ultimate plan is wrong and will leave you wounded and wanting what's real and right.

Got questions? Get answers. Go to the Bible for answers to your questions, and then go to God in prayer and ask him to help you avoid temptation, live according to his Word, and follow the leading of the Holy Spirit.

Your question: _____

Biblical comeback: _____

How it applies to your situation: _____

Write a prayer to God asking him to help. _____

_____

_____

_____

FYI

Learning to rely on your heavenly Father can be difficult if you have had a parent run out on you or abuse you. You may have a hard time imagining a loving, caring relationship with God the Father when your earthly father or mother or both parents have let you down, but know this—that God will never disappoint you.

What's It 2U?

Fatherly advice from God the Father is without a doubt the best advice you'll ever receive. The Bible has been tested and proven over and over again, and it has yet to fail anyone who has trusted it and applied it to their lives. The same Scripture that was good for your parents

Tammy's Tip

The ultimate good news is: God loves you no matter what and, nothing you can do will make God stop loving and caring for you.

is good for you too. Sure, generations change and technology moves forward, but God's Word stands the test of time, being superior to anything man has to offer.

So what does that mean to you? Well, for starters, God's Word says to save sex for marriage, even though society advances the opposite by emphasizing various forms of birth control and means of abortion. Remember, it's Satan who warps advice, making what the world has to offer seem updated and what God has to offer outdated, yet God's good old-fashioned advice consistently works in all situations.

Time Out
with Tammy

Alexis was just twelve years old when I met her. She arrived late to my Sunday school class, and while I was standing at the front of the room teaching, she stood in the back hunched over, appearing to stare at the floor, with her long, matted hair hiding her face. I interrupted the lesson to welcome her, gave her a book, and asked her to join us. Alexis never spoke a word as she took a seat, cowering like a scared little puppy who'd just been scolded. Once the Bible study was over, I made an attempt to warm up to her, but I soon realized it wasn't going to be easy as she coldly rejected every attempt I made to be her friend. No matter how hard I tried, she tried harder to ignore me. What was it with this girl? It was like one minute she would be on the verge of opening up and then the next minute she'd automatically shut down again. Months went by and she never missed a Sunday, yet she never got involved either. Finally one day she called me crying and almost yelling from the other end of the phone, "How can you say God loves and cares for me when he doesn't? You're a liar—if he really cared for me, then my mom would come back for me!" And with that she hung up.

That evening I went to visit Alexis and was greeted at the door by her grandfather. He told me Alexis wasn't home but asked if he could talk to me. He said, "Lexie loves you. She talks about you all the time. She can't wait to go to that church house on Sundays just to see you." I was a little puzzled to say the least, but then he continued, "I suppose you've been wondering where Lexie's parents are?" I said, "Yes, the thought had crossed my mind." And then he told me the story behind Alexis.

"Lexie's parents were divorced a couple of years ago, and my son (Lexie's dad) moved across country and started another family. Lexie and her younger sister

$C4$ Yourself

You may sometimes find this hard to accept, but your parents are not perfect. They've made mistakes and will continue to do so, and so will you. Your parents will disappoint and fail you, but God the Father will come through for you every time. He won't let you down, not even for a minute. You are your heavenly Father's daughter! Remembering who you ultimately belong to is essential, especially if you are like Alexis and have had a parent do you wrong. It's when we find

Katie lived with their mom. Then a few months back I came home to find Lexie sitting on my doorstep with a garbage bag full of clothes and stuff. I called her mama to see what was going on and why she had driven nearly six hours to bring Lexie and not brought Katie. And what she said was she couldn't stand lookin' at Lexie another day because she looked too much like her father, and so she was keepin' Katie and I could have Lexie."

I stood there dumbfounded, but I finally understood Alexis's odd behavior.

Nearly a year passed before Alexis trusted anyone to be her friend, including God, but one evening she opened up and let God and the rest of us into her world. It took time for her to work through her emotional anguish and her extreme fear of rejection.

The good news is: With God's help, Alexis came to trust in God's faithfulness and was even able to forgive her mother.

The bad news is: Alexis still struggles with the fear of rejection.

But more good news is: She uses her apprehension to reach out to others who suffer with the same anxiety.

Alexis is not alone. Many of us have been abandoned, abused, or alienated by our earthly parents, but don't let that affect how you respond to God the Father. He loves and cares for you more than you can comprehend, and he wants to help you with whatever it is you're going through.

ourselves in a tough situation that we wonder, "Where's God now?" The truth is, God never went anywhere; it's people who moved away from God. Sin corrupted the world, and as a result we live in a less than perfect civilization. So how can we make things better when everything seems hopeless?

You can only blame your parents for so long, and then it's up to you to decide what you will learn from them. Will you repeat their mistakes, or will you learn from them, changing the course of your future? You can't hold your parents responsible for your mistakes, and they can't hold you responsible for theirs either. Ultimately you own your choices and the repercussions that follow, good or bad.

● ● ● ● ● ● ● ● ● ● ● ● ● ● ● ● ● ●
**Be TRUE to YOU—Live
and learn today so that
you can lead tomorrow.**

Tammy's Tip

Our earthly parents are human and affected by sin, just like you and me, but God, our heavenly Father, is perfect. He makes no mistakes but instead saves us from them.

Alternative Lifestyles

Out of the Closet

Today we are challenged with far more than boys when it comes to dating and sex. We're also confronted with same-sex relationships. In the last few years homosexual and bisexual relationships have "come out of the closet," making us wonder who we are and how we fit into the sexual lineup. Am I gay, am I straight, or am I both? Society says one thing and Scripture says another, so how do we know what to believe or why to believe it?

Is it true that people are born with different sexual preferences? If you prefer to hang with your girlfriends instead of dating guys, does that mean you have homosexual tendencies? Television and school may teach acceptance of alternative lifestyles, yet your parents and church may denounce the gay rights movement, so what are you supposed to think?

In this final chapter I want to shed some light on sexual orientation and answer your questions on the subject. With so many messages out there stating what's right and what's wrong, how can you know for sure? Are you confused on the sexuality issue? Then please read on and allow me to clear things up for you.

When I was in grade school I acted "gay"—meaning happy, merry, light-hearted, and carefree—as I skipped home from school. When I was in junior high I acted "queer"—funny or odd in my own unique way. But by the time I was in high school, homosexuality had crept out of the closet, and being "gay" or "queer" took on a whole new definition, one I didn't want to be associated with. My, how times have changed! No wonder all the confusion. When definitions change, so does the explanation.

Since that time something else has changed, and that's choice. When I was growing up I was given the opportunity to decide whether or not I wanted to accept others' lifestyles as legitimate, but today you are not. In this day and age we are bombarded with acceptance. We are not given the opportunity to disagree without being labeled bigots.

Matter of Fact

The fact is, I'm not a bigot and I don't discriminate; I just don't happen to agree with same-sex relationships. Does that make me a homophobe? Not at all. I can't stand liver and I don't enjoy opera, but does that make me a liver-phobe or anti–opera singers? Hardly. I just don't happen to believe liver or opera should be thrust upon me in such a way that I'm made to accept them as a part of my life. So what does that have to do with homosexual or bisexual relationships? I should be given the right to accept or deny those types of lifestyles according to my own convictions without being labeled "intolerant," and being discriminated against for my belief.

Get a Clue

I want to clue you in to basic facts that will help you make your own choice on the topic of alternative lifestyles. The first fact is that God is the originator of choice. He gave us the right to choose from the get-go. Look back to the Garden

Tammy's Tip

What is the difference between disagreement and discrimination? Disagreement is a difference of opinion—a failure to agree. Discrimination is disagreeing simply based on hatred, bigotry, or prejudice. Although the definitions are similar it's hatred for the person or persons you disagree with that turns a disagreement into discrimination.

of Eden and you'll discover that Adam and Eve were given options from the very start. The question is, does that make every choice right? The answer is no, because preferences must fit with godly principles that lead to knowing what's right and what's wrong in the big scheme of things.

To help you know where you stand, I have compiled a list of arguments, answers, and applications concerning the alternative lifestyle movement. Use the following information to make an informed choice.

Argument: Aren't people born gay?

Answer: No scientific research exists that supports the theory that people are born as homosexuals. However, conclusive evidence does show that some people have stronger same-sex tendencies than others, and depending on environmental factors (such as parental, social, and experimental influences), some of those tendencies are acted upon and others are not.

Application: People are born with different tendencies. Some have the propensity to play basketball, some can easily play the piano, and still others have an artistic flair, but if those inclinations are not practiced and developed through outside influences, chances are they will not become part of the person's way of life.

Argument: Same-sex couples have the right to get married.

Answer: Gay rights have been compared to civil rights, but how do the two relate? Civil rights are about being denied basic privileges due to the color of your skin, your gender, or your religious affiliation. They are about the right to vote, work, and live without legal segregation; in short, they are about promoting unity, not division. Gay rights, on the other hand, segregate a class of people by their personal preference and then demand special allowances to accommodate their way of life. The fact is, preference indicates that one thing is more desirable to an individual than another thing, which would indicate to me that special interests are not a reason to create special laws to meet individual desires. What do I mean? Keep reading.

Application: Where do rights begin and end? What about the pet lover who considers his precious little poochie as his child? Should such a person be given preferential treatment such as the right to a legal, binding adoption in a court of law so he becomes an official "parent" to his pet, granted with parental benefits such as specialized veterinary health care provided by his employer? How far should the government go to satisfy individual choice? People from all walks of life prefer different things; some pets to people, some rock music to country music, some diet sodas to regular, etc., but that doesn't mean individual preference should be granted specialized privileges under the guise of civil rights. Remember, civil rights unite, but in this case, gay rights divide by sanctioning the singling out of a group of people based on choice.

Argument: What's wrong with an alternative lifestyle?

Answer: First, living an alternative lifestyle should be left up to the person or persons involved, without violating what I believe. For example, if I own a condo and decide to rent it out, and should a same-sex couple wish to rent it, I cannot turn them away because of their preferred lifestyle, even though it goes against my religious belief. Second, I'm concerned about the radical change of the definition of marriage. Same-sex marriage goes against the Bible's description of marriage as found in Matthew 19:4–5: "And [Jesus] answered and said to them, 'Have you not read that He who made [them] at the beginning "made them male and female," and said, "For this reason a man shall leave his father and mother and be joined to his wife, and the two shall become one flesh"?'" And Ephesians 19:5: "As the Scriptures say, 'A man leaves his father and mother and is joined to his wife and the two are united as one'" (NLT). Third, I'm not only concerned about how a married couple is defined, but I'm also concerned about the definition of a family. No longer will the nucleus of a family be just father, mother, and children, but instead we must adopt the idea of two dads raising children or two moms raising a family. Studies have indicated that children raised by homosexual couples lack confidence, independence, and security and are at a greater risk of gender confusion (this info is from Glenn T. Stanton, director of social research and cultural affairs and senior analyst for marriage and sexuality at Focus on the Family, and author of *Why Marriage Matters*).

Application: The alternative lifestyle of same-sex relationships is a relatively high-risk lifestyle. Sure, birth control is not an issue since it's physically impossible for a same-sex couple to procreate, but other risks are higher with same-sex activity. For example, the chances of getting sexually transmitted diseases such as HIV, hepatitis B, syphilis, or herpes is 57 percent with same-sex activity compared with 13 percent for heterosexual activity. These are serious risks that are rarely mentioned when alternative lifestyles are discussed. (Statistics taken from www.lifeissues.net, Dr. Michael Jarmulowicz.)

Simplify

So the question now is, "How do same-sex relationships apply directly or indirectly to you?" Find the answers you're looking for in the following true-to-life situations, which, for your benefit, are written as question and answer scenarios.

QUESTION: When I was in grade school a couple of my girlfriends and I watched a talk show (that I wasn't suppose to watch) about strippers. Afterwards we went in my friend's bedroom, locked the door, put on some music, and then took turns parading up and down the bed stripping while the other two sat on the floor and whistled and cheered. A couple of times we even grabbed each other, pretending to be men wanting more. After that day we never did it again, and we never talked about what we had done, but I can't help wondering if this means that deep down inside I'm attracted to girls, even though I think I like guys. How do I know if I might be a lesbian?

ANSWER: Curiosity does not make you a homosexual, and as I explained earlier, we have no reliable proof that people are born gay. What happened to you happens to many people— you were in the wrong place at the wrong time and as a result did something you wouldn't normally have done. Confusion is just one tactic that Satan uses to try to trick us into turning away from God's perfect plan. Ease your conscience by praying to ask God's forgiveness and then asking him to clear things up regarding your sexuality.

QUESTION: My boyfriend recently told me that it really turns him on to watch two girls making out and asked me to French kiss his friend Stan's girlfriend while the two of them watched. At first I said no, but then he kept pestering me until I finally gave in. Is it wrong to do something like this for your boyfriend's sake? What's wrong with kissing another girl? Britney Spears and Madonna kissed, and they're obviously not gay, but does this mean I could be bi?

ANSWER: Kissing another girl does not make you bisexual; however, it could definitely open the door to

Tammy's Tip

Remember, when you don't make a choice, your choice has been made for you.

that type of lifestyle. With today's growing trend to try an alternative way of life, bisexuality and three-way relationships have become socially acceptable in many circles and even encouraged as a way to experiment with both sexes so you can decide for yourself which you prefer. Is it wrong? Yes. Again, it leads to confusion, which is one of Satan's greatest weapons against us. Is it wrong if you're only doing it to please your boyfriend? Most definitely yes! Any guy that makes such a selfish request of you does not have your best interests in mind, only his. As far as Britney and Madonna are concerned, they are all about shocking society so that they can keep their names in the forefront of the media to help them sell more products.

QUESTION: I have a teacher who is a lesbian. She is my favorite teacher of all time. She's so nice and she has a real love for teaching. You can tell she enjoys her job and that she's not just there to collect a paycheck. I enjoy spending time with her. Sometimes I eat lunch with her in her classroom, and other times I stay after school to help her grade papers. The problem is, though, people at school are teasing me and calling me her "lesbo" partner. Does having a special feeling for my teacher mean she's rubbing off on me and I'm turning gay?

ANSWER: The answer is no. Liking one teacher over another does not mean you are gay even if she is. Each one of us at one time or another has someone we look up to in life. Just be careful not to allow this person to change you from who God created you to be. Sometimes it's easy to allow yourself to become confused by affection, admiration, and acceptance from another individual. People have been known to fall into dangerous situations because of emotional attachment, so beware. As far as your peers go, remember, kids are cruel. They are always looking for someone to tease, if for no other reason than to keep the taunting away from themselves.

QUESTION: My dad left my mom for a man when I was seven years old. As a result I would spend every other weekend with my dad and his partner. I'm now thirteen and just found out that my dad (who moved away a couple of years ago) is dying of AIDS and that his partner tested HIV-positive. I feel guilty that my dad is dying of AIDS because when he first left us for another man I hated him and wished he were dead because of the humiliation he put our family through. My question is, my dad says he's a Christian, but is it possible for him to be a Christian and a homosexual? I want him to go to heaven but I'm afraid he won't. I'm also worried that I could have contracted HIV during the time I spent with them when I was younger. My mom took me to the doctor and had me tested, and the test came back negative, but someone else told me that HIV doesn't always show up right away. Is that true?

ANSWER: First, let me say that I'm sorry about your father. What he did to you and your family is wrong, but he is still your dad, and I know that beneath the shame, disappointment, and anger you love and care for him deeply, and so does God. If your dad did indeed pray to receive Christ as his Lord and Savior, then yes, he is a Christian and yes, he will spend eternity in heaven. Homosexuality is a sin, but God always forgives those who repent.

With so much confusion out there about HIV/AIDS, let's make it clear how it is and isn't transmitted. HIV isn't transmitted by the kind of contact you'd normally have with someone you live with; without sexual activity, shared needles, or blood contact having taken place, you shouldn't have to worry. As far as HIV testing goes, negative test results indicate no antibodies to HIV were found. That means either 1) the person is not infected, 2) the test has been done before antibodies have been produced (which can take 3–6 months from the time the person was infected with the virus; however 96 percent of the time HIV shows up in a matter of weeks), or 3) the antibody levels were too low to be detected. A person who has been involved in risky behavior should be tested

Tammy's Tip

God does not play favorites. He hates *all* sin and loves *all* sinners.

again later to be sure, but in your case you have nothing to worry about since you had only casual contact with those who are HIV positive. (You can read more about this from the website of the McKinley Health Center at the University of Illinois at Urbana-Champaign, www.mckinley.uiuc.edu/health-info/sexual/stds/hiv-qaa.html, or www.aids.org/info/testing.html.)

FYI

All of us need to apply a godly outlook in order to deal with people who are different from us. God calls us to love the sinner and hate the sin. People who tease, mock, avoid, look down upon, or act violently against homosexuals are wrong. Christians are called to first love God and then love people regardless of their sin. This doesn't mean that we should condone their behavior or conform to it, but it does mean that we should care for the individual without a condescending attitude.

Quite often Christians are guilty of treating homosexuals as though they have participated in an unforgivable sin; however, according to the Bible only one sin is unforgivable, and that is rejecting the Holy Spirit of God.

I tell you that any sinful thing you do or say can be forgiven. Even if you speak against the Son of Man [Jesus] you can be forgiven. But if you speak against the Holy Spirit, you can never be forgiven, either in this life or in the life to come.

Matthew 12:31–32 CEV

All of us are sinners (see Rom. 3:23) and God does not categorize sin—so neither should we. How can we expect to introduce nonbelievers to a loving relationship with Christ when we, as believers, do not demonstrate his love? Try to live God's way and demonstrate God's love in all you say and do. And remember, just because you accept the person for who they are doesn't mean you are accepting what they do.

What's It 2U?

Some public schools have introduced the homosexual agenda into their required curriculum. They may teach you about same-sex relationships, making them appear commonplace, secure, and healthy, yet not all of what they communicate to you is true. For example, homosexuality is not as widespread as the media and gay special interest groups would have you believe. The fact is, same-sex relationships are now out in the open and talked about much more than in years past, which makes homosexuality seem much more commonplace.

Bottom line, you have the right to the truth about what you're being taught. You need to be able to make an informed decision, whether it's about an alternative lifestyle or something else that will affect your generation and generations to come. Don't sit idly by and let other people tell you what to think. Be smart. Gather all the facts. Compare them to the Word of God, and then judge for yourself.

C4 Yourself

I want you to see for yourself what the Word of God has to say about homosexual and bisexual behavior. You might be surprised by what it says and how it says it. To make it a little easier to under-

Tammy's Tip

A self-righteous attitude toward the unrighteous is not all right, but a loving attitude toward them demonstrates God's love, so maybe they'll realize their need and get right with God. Remember, we're called to love the sinners not the sin.

stand, I've broken it down into a past, present, and future outline that describes 1) God's original plan, 2) his current view, and 3) his future judgment.

Past

Physical intimacy was designed by God to bring a man and a woman together as one flesh in holy matrimony.

> Jesus answered, "Don't you know that in the beginning the Creator made a man and a woman? That's why a man leaves his father and mother and gets married. He becomes like one person with his wife. Then they are no longer two people, but one. And no one should separate a couple that God has joined together."
>
> Matthew 19:4–6 CEV

Although Jesus was addressing divorce in this portion of Scripture, he also stated God's original plan for marriage—a man becomes one with his wife. Nowhere in the Bible does God condone same-sex relationships. God only recognizes marriages between one man and one woman. Anything else is wrong in the eyes of God.

Present

God always has and always will condemn any type of sexual behavior other than that between husband and wife.

> Don't have sex with a man as one does with a woman. That is abhorrent.
>
> Leviticus 18:22 Message

> That is why God abandoned them to their shameful desires. Even the women turned against the natural way to have sex and instead indulged in sex with each other. And the men, instead

of having normal sexual relationships with women, burned with lust for each other. Men did shameful things with other men and, as a result, suffered within themselves the penalty they so richly deserved.

Romans 1:26–27 NLT

Plain and simple, homosexual behavior is loathed by God. Such perversion destroys God's plan for marriage; it distorts the oneness God intended between man and woman and the ability to procreate. However, not all is lost, because God offers mercy and forgiveness to everyone.

Future

According to Scripture, people can change their lifestyles. God gives everyone the benefit of his grace and guidance to do so.

Don't you know that evil people won't have a share in the blessings of God's kingdom? Don't fool yourselves! No one who is immoral or worships idols or is unfaithful in marriage or is a pervert or behaves like a homosexual will share in God's kingdom. . . . Some of you used to be like that. But now the name of our Lord Jesus Christ and the power of God's Spirit have washed you and made you holy and acceptable to God.

1 Corinthians 6:9–11 CEV

Everything a person says or does is driven by his or her own will. Only after we confess our sins and conform our will to God's will (instead of trying to conform God to ours) will we experience true change from the inside out. Our bodies belong to God, and as believers we should glorify him through our bodies.

Life can be confusing. We are bombarded with propaganda from all directions, yet we have only one alternative to these

Alternative Lifestyles

alternative lifestyles, and that is living God's way. Allow God to be your guide and you'll end up on the right track.

> Trust God from the bottom of your heart; don't try to figure out everything on your own. Listen for God's voice in everything you do, everywhere you go; he's the one who will keep you on track. Don't assume that you know it all. Run to God! Run from evil!
>
> Proverbs 3:5–7 Message

Closet Christians

One thing I've noticed over the last few years is that as sin advances, Christians retreat, and as sinful lifestyles become acceptable, Christianity becomes unacceptable. It's like sin comes out of the closet and we move into the closet, hoping not to be exposed for who we are in Christ, and it's all driven by fear of rejection. It's not that we're ashamed of who we are; it's just that we're afraid to take a stand. We're made to feel singled out and alone when various groups, like those of the gay rights movement, claim a great number of supporters. In fact, sometimes we become so intimidated that we take on the opinion, "If you can't beat 'em . . . learn to live with it." Our response becomes, "I wouldn't do it myself, but I can't judge what's right for someone else." But the truth of the matter is, you can. God's Word clearly distinguishes between right and wrong. You can either choose to sit back and idly agree to disagree, or you can take a stand for what's right in the eyes of God.

Christians, unite! Let your voice be heard. You are the next generation. You will be given the right to vote, to make or rewrite laws, and to influence the future for the better or worse. It's all about coming together as God's children and

God offers an alternative to those seeking an alternative lifestyle.

living out loud for him. Live in a way that will make others see God living in you and want the same godly alternative lifestyle that you've accepted for yourself.

Matter of Fact

I know all the things you do, that you are neither hot nor cold. I wish you were one or the other! But since you are like lukewarm water, I will spit you out of my mouth!

Revelation 3:15–16 NLT

God would rather that you deny him altogether than acknowledge him but act like he doesn't mean anything to you. He wants your all or nothing.

It's like when I order a soda, I want it ice cold. That's when it's refreshing. Or if I order regular coffee, I want it piping hot so that when I take a sip I feel rejuvenated. On the flip side, if I receive a soda or coffee that's lukewarm, you can forget it, I don't want it. That's how it is with God: he'd rather we be ice cold to him or on fire for him than somewhere in between.

Get a Life

God wants your loyalty to be to him first and foremost. He wants you to represent him in the choices you make. God wants to be your best friend, not only when it's convenient (like when you want something) but now and always, in the good times and in the bad. He'll never leave you, and he doesn't want you to skip out on him either.

God does not want halfhearted Christians. He wants all of you. You can't live as if you're committed only at your convenience and expect God to bless you in your choices.

The alternative to accepting Jesus
is receiving God's judgment.

You can't serve God and self—but you can serve yourself by
serving God.

> If you serve Christ in this way, you will please God and be re-
> spected by people.
>
> Romans 14:18 CEV

Standing your ground whether or not people agree with you
will earn you respect. Even though my fellow biology students
didn't agree with me on creation, many of them expressed that
they thought it was cool that I was unashamed to stand up
for what I believed in. A couple of students even confessed to
me that they didn't agree with evolution but were too afraid
to admit it. Bottom line: don't sell out due to fear of rejection,
but stand firm in your faith and be approved by God.

> Do your best to win God's approval as a worker who doesn't
> need to be ashamed and who teaches only the true message.
>
> 2 Timothy 2:15 CEV

Time Out
with Tammy

When I was a freshman in high school I took biology. Toward the end of the year
the biology teacher, Mr. Fish, announced that we would be studying evolution as
the last unit of study before the year-end final examination. He acknowledged the
fact that not all of us would agree with the theory but asked that we keep an open
mind during the lesson and said that at the end of the study we would be given the
opportunity to debate the idea. Up until that point I had found biology so-so, but
now it was about to become a challenge, and I love challenges. Over the next
several days I listened intently to what was being taught so that I could prepare for
the big debate. I took the data and then used the Bible to blow holes in Mr. Fish's
theory (which coincidently stated that we evolved from fish).

The day of the debate I was ready. I had enlisted a couple of friends to stand with
me on the side of creationism. However, on the day of the great debate one girl
took a look at the odds, which were 21 to 3 (we were the 3) and bailed to the
opposing side, which by the way included Mr. Fish. Once the debate started it was

The fear [love, respect, and obedience] of the LORD is the beginning of wisdom.

Proverbs 9:10 NIV

The Simple Truth

Following Christ is not always easy. Many times we are pushed by our friends to do something we know we shouldn't do, and then we're faced with the decision, "Will I do what Jesus would do, or will I do what my friends want me to do?" And the truth is, doing what's right can make you feel left out, teased, and very much alone, but on the flip side of that, following your friends can make you feel alienated from God.

Keep your conscience clear. Then if people speak evil against you, they will be ashamed when they see what a good life you live because you belong to Christ. Remember, it is better to suf-

basically me against a couple other students, but once I started winning, Mr. Fish jumped in, and it came down to the two of us. I kept waiting for my ally to back me up, but she sat there like a bump on a log, not saying a word. Finally Mr. Fish got so frustrated with me that he ordered me to the office, and even then my friend didn't say a word in my defense. She just sat there and allowed me to go to the principal's office and take a zero on that unit of study, and she even let the teacher get away with saying, "There's just no talking to you closed-minded Christians." Honestly, I was wishing she hadn't chosen to be on my side since she wasn't willing to back me up and openly defend God's creation.

Have you ever had a friend like that, the kind of person who was with you until the rubber met the road and then bailed? It makes you kind of sick, doesn't it? Well, it's of poor taste to God too; it makes him sick enough to (figuratively) spit you out (see Rev. 3:15–16)!

fer for doing good, if that is what God wants, than to suffer for
doing wrong!

1 Peter 3:16–17 NLT

If you experience rejection as a Christian, don't feel alone,
because Christ experienced it first.

If you find the godless world is hating you, remember it got
its start hating me. If you lived on the world's terms, the world
would love you as one of its own. But since I picked you to live
on God's terms and no longer on the world's terms, the world is
going to hate you.

John 15:18–19 Message

Living as a Christian isn't always easy. People are preju-
diced against our faith and taunt, tease, and persecute those
involved. Being a Christian is filled with everyday challenges;
however, the payoff is worth the harassment. Accepted or
not, "I'm only passing through; this world is not my home."
The key is to avoid shortsightedness by basing today's decisions on eternity.

God blesses those who are persecuted because they live for
God, for the Kingdom of Heaven is theirs. God blesses you
when you are mocked and persecuted and lied about because
you are my followers. Be happy about it! Be very glad! For a
great reward awaits you in heaven. And remember, the ancient
prophets were persecuted, too.

Matthew 5:10–12 NLT

Doing the right thing and standing up for what you believe in can leave you feeling outnumbered, but remember:
You + God = the Majority. Vote with God and you always
win. So the next time you're tempted by the fear of rejection, pray and ask God to strengthen your commitment to

him and give you courage to overcome the temptation to compromise.

> Be of good courage, and He shall strengthen your heart, all you who hope in the LORD.
>
> Psalm 31:24 NKJV

FYI

You can make a difference. Let your voice be heard. You've got the power to make things happen and influence change. Voting is not just a right but also a responsibility, and although you may not be of voting age yet, you can still get involved in the political process.

Inform yourself on the issues that affect you and then look for ways to take action. Do you see a problem with school policy? You have the right to address the school board. Does something need to be changed in your community? Write to your local officials or the editor of your local newspaper, or attend a city council meeting. Maybe the issue is violence, gay rights, illegal skateboarding, the right to life, or something else—whatever your concerns may be, freedom of speech is your right. Use your voice to educate others. Remember, involvement influences change.

You can make a difference, and here's how:

EDUCATE yourself on the issues

ENCOURAGE other young people to get involved

ENLIST fellow supporters (such as with the use of a petition)

ENDORSE what you believe in

ELECT those who support your beliefs or, if

Tammy's Tip

When you've been invaded by the Holy Spirit, you've got the power!

you are not of voting age yet, support your candidate any way you can

Participation is power and God on our side is empowerment, but we can't make a difference if we don't get involved. Exercise your rights, or else you may lose them.

Make the Master proud of you by being good citizens. Respect the authorities, whatever their level; they are God's emissaries for keeping order. It is God's will that by doing good, you might cure the ignorance of the fools who think you're a danger to society. Exercise your freedom by serving God, not by breaking the rules. Treat everyone you meet with dignity. Love your spiritual family. Revere God. Respect the government.

1 Peter 2:13–17 Message

What's It 2𝒰?

You have been set apart by God. He has enlisted you in his army. You have been called to love God and to love others as yourself, including both those who love you back and those who loathe the ground you walk on.

But I say, love your enemies! Pray for those who persecute you! In that way, you will be acting as true children of your Father in heaven. For he gives his sunlight to both the evil and the good, and he sends rain on the just and on the unjust, too. If you love only those who love you, what good is that? . . . If you are only kind to your friends, how are you different from anyone else?

Matthew 5:44–47 NLT

We can easily love people we have something in common with, but loving those who are different from us goes against the norm. Only through the power of the Holy Spirit living in us are we able to replace hatred with a compassion for love. Christians are called to do what's *not* humanly possible, but that's the cool part, because God will enable you to do what you can't do on your own.

I challenge you to pray for one of your enemies today, and instead of asking God to change that person, ask him to change your attitude toward that person. It won't be easy at first, but trust me, it works. A few years ago I harbored a mean-spirited dislike toward homosexuals and everything they stood for, but then God convicted me about my un-Christlike mind-set. I prayed and asked God to forgive me for my attitude and help me correct it. I prayed to grow in care and compassion for individuals and to have the ability to separate what people do physically from who they are spiritually. And you know what? I succeeded. God has helped me strip off the sin and see the soul. It's all about looking past the outside into the condition of a person's heart, and when you do that, you'll discover that all of us have one thing in common: *YOU, ME, EVERYBODY—WE ALL NEED JESUS!*

God wants everyone to be saved and to know the whole truth, which is, there is only one God, and Christ Jesus is the only one who can bring us to God.

1 Timothy 2:4–5 CEV

C4 Yourself

You are your future. Many of your ideas about tomorrow are being shaped today. It's up to you to decide what you value and where you're going to place your faith—either in

Tammy's Tip

One way you can do your part is to encourage everyone you know who is of voting age to support laws that reflect God's ways and then get out there and VOTE.

the ways of God or in the ways of man, because the fact is, you can't have it both ways. Keep in mind that temporary acceptance comes from man and eternal acceptance comes from God. You must decide for yourself who you are going to serve and then stand on your convictions. Your voice matters and can make a difference. Don't let fear shut you up, but live out loud for God. Remember, God handpicked you to represent him—to live, love, and lead people to eternal life for him.

> You did not choose me. I chose you and sent you out to produce fruit, the kind of fruit that will last. Then my Father will give you whatever you ask in my name. So I command you to love each other.
>
> John 15:16–17 CEV

Choose this day whom you will serve, and when it's all said and done you will be able to live with your choices.

● ●

Be TRUE to YOU—Live life out loud,
loving others through the Lord Jesus Christ.

Tammy's Tip

Hatred heads people to hell.
Love leads people to the Lord.

Conclusion

Worth the Wait

I hope this book has given you insight into what purity is all about. It's not just a physical state but also a state of mind. As you enter the wide world of guys, dating, and sex you have to decide how you're going to handle yourself so it doesn't handle you. It's all about self-control through prayer and practice.

As your friend and as a mom, I want to encourage you to play it safe and to protect your purity at all costs. And as a sister in Christ I also want to remind you to hold onto God's promises.

You are God's precious daughter. He treasures you no matter what you've done in the past. Today is a new day with new possibilities for better tomorrows. It's your privilege and prerogative as a young woman to pursue God's best for you.

Love from your Big Sis,

Tammy

Thanks to You

Dear Father,

I dedicate this book to you. I pray that you would use it to purify the hearts and minds of those who read it so that they may become more Christlike each and every day.

And I thank you, God and Father, for allowing me to be the pen in your hand. I dedicate this book to your plan and purpose.

Dear Family and Friends,

Thank you for inspiring me to be all that I can be through the Lord Jesus Christ. Your love, support, and prayers have been my source of encouragement from the very start. I love you, I love you, I love you! You're the greatest!

> To my high school sweetheart and husband, Ed: I thank God for you. You are my soul mate, the light of my life, and the wind beneath my wings. xoxox
>
> To Matt and Ash: I'm so proud of both of you. I'm praying for God to give you his wisdom, protection, and nurturing as you strike off on your own to find your place in this world. I love you!
>
> To Dad and Mom: Thank you for loving one another and instilling in me the value of growing old with a godly spouse. I love you!
>
> To my girlfriends: Thank you for teaching me the value of godly girlfriends. Your love and honesty keep me humble but happy!
>
> To my church family: Thank you for listening and for lifting me up before the throne.
>
> To the moms who shared their hearts: Thank you for making yourselves vulnerable on a very intimate subject.
>
> To you, my reader: I hope you have enjoyed this book. I'd love to hear your thoughts and answer any questions you might have. Please email me at MakeOverMin@aol.com.

Tammy Bennett's background in design, fashion, cosmetics, television, and modeling has served as a springboard for her writing and speaking. As a staff member for Upper CLASS, she teaches others how to be effective communicators through the use of color, clothing, and cosmetics. She frequently speaks to young girls (including her own teenage daughter) on the subject of enhancing beauty. Tammy and her family live in Newark, Delaware.

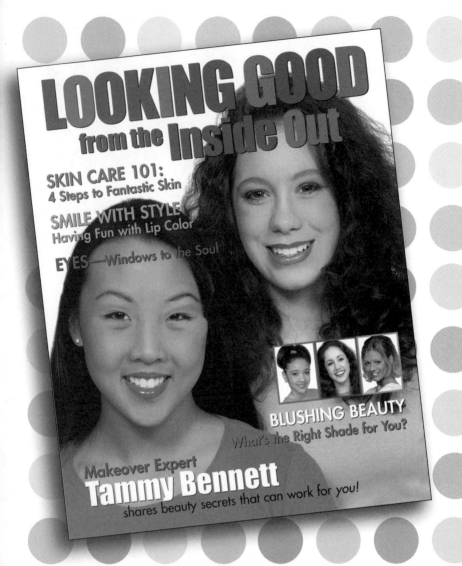

LOOKING GOOD
from the Inside Out

SKIN CARE 101:
4 Steps to Fantastic Skin

SMILE WITH STYLE
Having Fun with Lip Color

EYES—Windows to the Soul

BLUSHING BEAUTY
What's the Right Shade for You?

Makeover Expert
Tammy Bennett
shares beauty secrets that can work for you!

From skin care
to lipstick color . . .

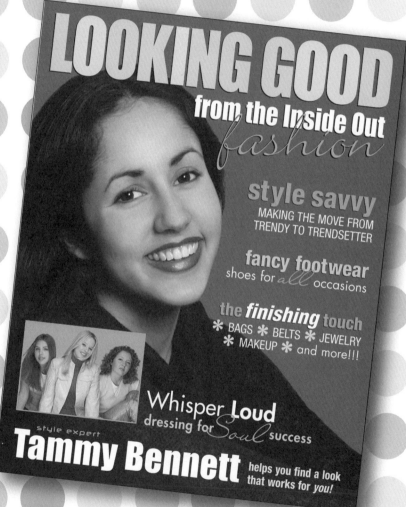

And secrets on inner beauty, too!

LOOKING GOOD
from the Inside Out
fashion

style savvy
MAKING THE MOVE FROM
TRENDY TO TRENDSETTER

fancy footwear
shoes for *all* occasions

the finishing touch
✱ BAGS ✱ BELTS ✱ JEWELRY
✱ MAKEUP ✱ and more!!!

Whisper Loud
dressing for *Soul* success

style expert
Tammy Bennett helps you find a look that works for *you!*

Available at your local bookstore

Ⓡ Revell